THE DONKEY RACE

OTHER BOOKS BY DIANA PULLEIN-THOMPSON
IN THE ARMADA SERIES INCLUDE

A PONY FOR SALE

HORSES AT HOME

JANET MUST RIDE

RIDING WITH THE LYNTONS

THREE PONIES AND SHANNAN

A PONY TO SCHOOL

I WANTED A PONY

THE PENNYFIELDS

© DIANA PULLEIN-THOMPSON 1958

The Donkey Race was first published in the U.K. in 1958 under the title The Boy and the Donkey by Wm. Collins Sons & Co. Ltd., London and Glasgow. This edition was first published in 1970 by May Fair Books Ltd., 14 St. James's Place, London, S.W.1, and was printed in Great Britain by Love & Malcomson Ltd., Brighton Road, Redhill, Surrey.

DIANA PULLEIN-THOMPSON

The Donkey Race

TEXT ILLUSTRATIONS BY SHIRLEY HUGHES

Armada

With love to Joanna Cannan,
in whose orchard a tired old donkey
spent the evening of her life

Chapter One

THE MAN and the donkey were at the corner again, the four-wheeled cart heavily laden with iron, rags and countless newspapers, when Duggie walked home from school between the terraces of high houses with peeling porticos and heavy paintless doors.

The donkey was small and grey with a white muzzle and a white covering to his stomach which would have looked like a shirt front had he stood up on his sturdy hind legs and walked like a man. He waited patiently, a humble expression in his brown eyes, while his master struggled to move the junk farther forward in the cart, and the first drips of rain came with the dusk and spattered on the empty road.

Duggie knew the old man was known as Old Jock and Duggie's mother had said he was a dishonest beggar best left alone. But the boy couldn't walk past and leave the bent figure struggling on his own. Besides, it seemed hard luck on the donkey, who must be getting hungry for his tea.

So Duggie stopped and asked whether he could lend a hand. And the old man straightened his back and said it wasn't often young people put themselves out these days. He stared at the boy with eyes which were an honest blue. There was nothing cunning about his face, so that Duggie doubted his mother's assertion.

"My back is awful bad with the lumbago. Seventy-seven I am this month. Och, it's hard work for an old man and no mistake. If you will be moving that piece

5

of iron, while I lift the sack of rags, I will be grateful to you. The donkey will be wanting his tea, too, seeing we were on the road at eight this morning." The man half-talked like a Scot and his voice had just the hint of a lilt in it.

Duggie helped him shift the junk, and learned that the donkey came from Ireland, was ten years old, and called Tam o' Shanter—Tammy for short.

"If you would like to come back with me, I will show you a photo of him when he came over, a pretty donkey he was then with a straight back."

They went down the street together to the narrow mews in which Tammy lived, and here in a stall there was the sweet smell of hay, and the pale gold of straw new from the wheat-fields of summer. Duggie felt he had come into a different quieter world, far removed from his home of two rooms, cluttered and noisy, occupied by his parents and his brother and sister as well as himself.

Presently Old Jock's terrier, Toby, came and sniffed round Duggie's legs and then the black and white cat, Flora, joined them, purring contentedly. It seemed like a farm in the midst of London to Duggie, whose great-grandfather had been a farm labourer and a fine hand with a plough and a team of horses. Old Jock had forgotten all about his promise to show Duggie the photograph and the boy didn't like to remind him because he seemed so old and breathless.

"Must be getting home. I can always help you after school," said Duggie at last, patting Tammy's neck and laughing at the flapping grey ears, the white-ringed eyes and the wide woolly cheeks . . . like a toy, stuffed animal for a kid of three, he thought, affectionately.

He remembered suddenly that he had promised to meet his best friend at school, Pete, after tea. They were going to explore a bomb site up by the Harrow

The man and the donkey were at the corner again

Road. Sometimes people found things like silver spoons and brooches in the ruins from the last war, and to-night Duggie and Pete were going to search the weeds, the broken bricks and mortar by torchlight.

"Better be going," he said again, edging towards the door.

"Come again, lad—always welcome," grunted Old Jock. "You're a strong one for your size. How old are you?"

"Ten. I'm small, but Mum says she used to be, too. And she's five feet six now. Shot up she says when she was thirteen, four inches in a year."

"You're all right. Now off you go," said Old Jock,

looking at the boy's fair hair, which crowned a pale face lit by speckled hazel eyes.

"O.K. Be seeing you. Bye, Tammy."

He ran out into the murky dusk. A few mellow lamps blinked gold into the damp darkness like low-hung stars. The tall houses closed in on either side, climbing upwards to meet the inky sky of night; here and there lights shone behind curtains; and shadows moved. Duggie took to his heels and ran to his more homely street, where the terraces were lower, two-storied, and without porticos or balconies, where women stood in their doorways looking out for their husbands, and scruffy dogs set out alone and independent for their evening walk.

He saw Mrs. Towers walking back from Jones, the grocer's.

"You'd better be running, Duggie, my boy, your Mum's after you. Been wanting you to pop up to the shop for some paraffin for the last half-hour. She'll skin you, she will," she called.

Soon he was in the kitchen and the gaslight was flickering, as gaslights do, and a tin kettle was boiling on the cooker, sending steam up against the walls which were dark green half-way up and then a dirty cream. There was warmth here and his mother was bending over the stone sink in her flowered smock with her hair in curlers, and Freddie was sniffing.

"What on earth's happened to you?" asked Duggie's mother. "I want some paraffin for the stove, seeing Jennie and Fred have colds . . . better have a bit of warmth in this kitchen. That cooker doesn't give off much, lord knows. Come on, here's the can. Off you go or Jones's will be shut."

"When are we going to have the other room, the one upstairs, like you said?" he asked. Suddenly he was tired of the squash, of trying to sleep while his

8

mother pottered about the kitchen and Dad came back, and Freddie sniffed. Miss Hamburger had left the room above them last week and gone into a home for the aged. The landlord had promised them her room for the two boys to sleep in, and though Freddie didn't care, Duggie longed for the change.

"Monday. Now go and get that paraffin. You won't get your tea till you have," said Mrs. Brown.

He went out again into the night. Pete was there, and said, "Where have you been? I've got the torch."

"Down with Old Jock's donkey and the dog and the cat. I helped them, and I'm going again. I like it there."

"Down with the rag and bones? Bet it stank," said Pete.

"No, it was clean like the country, like that farm we went to on the outing, and he's a lovely donkey ... ten."

"Are you ready now to go to that site? I've got a trowel," said Pete, still unimpressed by Duggie's enthusiasm.

"Got to get some paraffin first. Freddie and Jennie are sniffing, and Dad's out." He looked at Pete's dark head, the long narrow face.

"Would you like to come and see Tammy tomorrow night?" he asked.

"Who's Tammy?"

"The donkey."

"Dad said he might give me enough for the flicks."

"O.K. I won't be a moment. Mum won't half be cross if I don't hurry up and get that perishing paraffin. Coming?"

"All right."

Fair and dark, the two boys hurried on to the broader busier road, where the lights were closer and brighter, and the cars came in an endless stream, and people hurried home from work, the blacks and the

9

whites, and the great red buses grunted and groaned as they stopped and started with their loads of workers. Pete was thinking of the bombed site. He felt the little trowel protruding from the pocket of his ragged shorts; he saw half-crowns beneath the decaying willow herb, glistening in the wet earth. Duggie was thinking of the little donkey, for he had always wanted an animal of his own, a cat or a dog, but his parents had no room to spare, not even a corner for a basket. Almost more he would have loved to ride. He had been to the White City and seen the jumping there. When I'm grown up I shall work on a farm, he decided. He thought of the soft-eyed Jersey cows he had seen on the outing, of the grey sheep with their woolly lambs, and of the stretching acres with never a house or a chimney in sight.

Chapter Two

"RAG O'BONE, rag o' bone!" Old Jock's hoarse voice rose above the distant roar of the traffic in Kensington High Street, the drip, drip of the December rain, the slamming of doors, the sharp click of the taxi meters. It reached the grey walls, penetrated the closed sash windows and returned to them as the next cry rose in his parched throat.

They were on their way home now. Duggie was happy walking beside the rain-sleekened donkey. The cart was three-quarters full, with rags making the majority of the load. Other rag-and-bone men used ponies for the job. Duggie wondered why Old Jock had a donkey instead. He supposed Tammy was cheap to feed, for he seemed to keep fat on incredibly little.

Mostly the man and the boy were silent, apart from that age-old shout. But it was a good companionable silence.

"Not done so badly," said Old Jock at last. "People are so flighty nowadays, don't want a few pence for their old clothes. Times have changed, lad, nothing's the same; nothing."

"It's a free life," Duggie said, not noticing the dirty side of the business. "I'll see what my Mum's got at home, but she's expecting another baby and sometimes it makes her impatient and tired, and I think we need all our old clothes."

He remembered her anger last night when he spilt the tea on the floor and he was glad he had been out all day with the man and the donkey.

"Don't you bother her," said Old Jock. "So you'll be having another brother or sister?"

They came out in the High Street, feeling very small beside the high buses, and making slow progress, for Tammy was a poor walker. A mounted policeman on a shining chestnut clattered by with a jingle of bit and stirrup. The rain seemed to double its efforts, coming much faster and in larger drops, and the smell of damp rags was with them, and the wet wood of the cart.

"Must try to keep the paper dry. Pull the mackintosh sheet farther forward, will you, Duggie lad? I'm going to the depot to-morrow. I've got more than a full load now with the stuff at home, and I will be picking up some hay for Tammy from Weltons on the way home. Time I retired. I'm getting old, lad, too old for walking in the rain I'm thinking."

"What will happen to Tammy then? You wouldn't

sell him? He's got used to you and Toby and the cat, and all."

Duggie patted the grey neck; the long ears flicked back; the narrow tail swished like the ragged end of a rope; the wise head nodded.

"Wonder what he'd be like to ride," he said.

"Going to get in the cart. I'm not quite myself to-day, I'm thinking . . . tired, weary, lad. Och, I should never have come to London. It's a damp sad place to be sure."

Duggie suddenly noticed the old man's face was as white as the sheets for sale in the shop they were passing, and his blue eyes glowed like jewels, and he panted like an old dog as he climbed into the gaily painted cart.

"Are you feeling bad? Those sacks are wet for you to sit on. Shall I get you a cup of tea quick? Tammy won't mind waiting a moment."

Tea was Mrs. Brown's remedy for all ills. "Pulls you together, a nice cup of tea," she would say, and her children had started the habit young.

Duggie could see an Espresso coffee bar, but the people inside didn't look his sort . . . students, he thought, educated people and artists; he could see most prominently a dark female head, dangling earrings and a fragile hand holding an ivory cigarette holder.

"Might get one there," he added doubtfully.

"No, we had best be getting back. I shall be feeling a wee bit better once I'm home. It's the rain and the cold and I walked too far," said Old Jock, turning up the dusty collar of the old herring-bone tweed coat.

He called no more and Duggie urged the little grey donkey into a trot and, not wishing to add to the load, ran beside the cart, and thus they came to Notting Hill Gate, where there was much congestion of traffic and children nudged their parents and said, "Look at that donkey and that boy. What are they doing?"

Old Jock thought of Arisaig, of the green-grey Sound and farther out the blue outlines of Rum and Eigg and Muck. He had come to London so long ago that he often failed to bring a clear picture of his homeland to his mind when this sudden nostalgia caught him and he needed it most. He succeeded now and felt sad; then his thoughts drifted to his Cockney wife who had died last spring. She had laughed sometimes at his Scottish lilt, and he had learned some of her words and ways, in the forty-five years they had been together. "A perishin' 'orrible day, dearie," she would have said, and been ready with the whisky bottle to revive him on his return. But those days were over. He looked at the fair-haired boy who had become miraculously his friend, and drove out the past.

"Too old," he muttered, "too old. Been about too long, that's the trouble. Going to be seventy-seven next April, Do you hear that, boy, seventy-seven?"

"You are the oldest person I know," said Duggie, looking back at the wrinkled face as though you could count the years there. "I'll manage Tammy when we get back. I know where everything lives, and Pete can help me. Don't you worry, mister."

The lamps were on, glowing like round golden balls through the driven rain, as they came down towards Ladbroke Grove. Few pedestrians were about and those were bent nearly double as though beaten by the storm. Cars splashed Tammy's legs with water but he was above noticing such minor discomforts. Ahead they could see the bright lights of a row of shops beyond the smeared, dripping window fronts. Doors opened, casting forth a sudden, brief yellow into the grey of dusk, and closed again.

13

The gritty smell of trains came to them and stayed in their throats, and they could hear the shunting and an occasional whistle from Paddington or Royal Oak. And the smoke from the station and from the houses came down with the rain and hung in the air like fog, so that they could hardly see their way when they left the big road, although it was barely four o'clock.

These seemed suddenly like his animals

"Wee glens they were and green hills, and we had a white cottage and the garden. Och, my father was proud of that garden. But times were bad and I went to Glasgow, and I was a wild lad. Och, there was never a wilder one," said Old Jock to the sacks and the paper, the old bedstead and the ragged clothing which filled the cart. "But when I met my Elsie there was no holding me—London it had to be. She was

14

enough to turn any lad's head. I was a young one, and a wilder one you never saw."

He's feeling funny to-day. Duggie thought as he puffed beside the donkey. He's never talked like that before. He's sick. I'll water and feed Tammy, and then I must find something for the dog and cat. And I mustn't be too long because I've promised to meet Pete. Mum won't half be cross when she sees me so perishin' wet.

"Nearly there," he said encouragingly to the figure crouching and muttering in the cart. "Only five minutes now."

They came to the mews at last; water was gurgling in the gutters and the drains, running wildly over the cobbles and beating on the tiles of the grey houses with an erratic tap-tap. Curtains were drawn against the night and windows were shut. Suddenly Duggie shivered with the eeriness and the cold and the loneliness. Don't know why I ever came, he thought, except there was nothing else to do and I love the donkey and the dog and the cat, and Old Jock's all right.

"I will feed and water Tammy, so you can go to your room. Okay?" he asked, and his voice seemed small and light and far away in contrast to this wild wet twilight which had come on them so suddenly.

"I'll see to the donkey first. Can't leave my old friend. He's done me well," said the old man, clambering slowly from the cart.

"I've told you I can see to him. I did it once before, didn't I? You're bad, mister, sick. You're white," said Duggie, and he couldn't keep a note of irritation out of his voice, because he knew he was capable of dealing with the donkey and he wanted to do so, and he was upset by Old Jock's appearance.

He began to unharness Tammy, and Toby came out of the stall and welcomed his master and, after a bit,

Old Jock said, "All right, Duggie, you're a fine lad and I'll leave it to you. But he's a very good donkey, to be sure, and if you do anything wrong I will not be forgiving you quickly."

"Have you got anything to eat and a shilling for the gas?" asked Duggie, mollified.

"Yes, and I've a drop of whisky, too, and that'll put a bit of warmth into my old bones, do me a power of good." Jock was mixing the words he had learned in England with his Highland talk now. "I had kept it for the New Year, but I'll not be thinking of that this evening."

He shuffled away without more ado to the great decaying houses which lined the road at the far end of the mews, in which he had his basement room. Duggie thought of him lighting the gas-ring, putting on the black kettle, hanging the wet coat on the hook on the back of the brown door.

The boy was happy drying Tammy with straw, as Old Jock had shown him last week, in the gentle glow cast by the single hurricane light. Behind him, Flora, pleased with his company, purred on the last truss of hay. In the doorway lay Toby, his little tail waving and his deep-brown eyes watching Duggie. These seemed suddenly like *his* animals and he began to think about the food for the dog and cat again. Old Jock was not himself or he would never have forgotten them, thought Duggie. If only he had some money he could nip round the corner to the shop to get something.

Chapter Three

"Where are you off to so early? I want you to pop up to Jones's at nine and get some cough sweets for our Jennie, seeing her throat's so bad," said Mrs. Brown, as Duggie put on his brown jacket which was getting a bit tight under the arms.

"Couldn't Freddie go? His cough's better to-day. I'm meeting someone," said the boy, watching his mother as she spread the best Danish butter on a thick slice of white bread.

"You're the eldest. You should be ashamed to leave things to your younger brother. Who are you meeting —Pete?" asked Mrs. Brown, settling more comfortably on the couch with her breakfast, biting into the butter.

He was tempted to lie. She wouldn't check that he was meeting his friend and she might be annoyed to learn he was going to help Old Jock. In the end he compromised.

"Jones's opens at half-past eight. I'll wait and go there first," he said, and he saw his mother's prominent white teeth bite into the creamy yellow butter—one of her extravagances. She always said she could feel it doing her good as she ate it. Dad was sleeping beyond.

He had been on the late shift. His coat was lying across the low arm-chair; it smelt of the railway. There was a line of grease round the inside rim of his cap. His shoes were just inside the door. He had taken them off, so as not to waken his wife as he crept behind into their room in the early hours of the morning.

Couldn't Freddie go?"

To-night I shall be sleeping upstairs, thought Duggie. And Jennie will be in here, instead of with Mum and Dad. I hope she won't be frightened. She was playing on the floor now—a fair-haired three-year-old with bright cheeks and strong little limbs, and a determination which startled them. She was the healthiest of the lot, Mrs. Brown said, and Duggie thought she was going to be pretty as well, with those blue eyes and curly locks and that smile which showed the even white teeth in the smooth pink gums.

Outside the sun was shining, and the storm of yesterday already seemed an impossibility for the skies were clear and cold and tranquil and the hoar from last night's frost still lay here and there on the walls.

Duggie whistled as he went for the sweets and thought of the donkey and the man, both suddenly his responsibility, and of the cat and dog which seemed to rely on him now; and he wondered whether they were all waiting for him, the donkey tied in the stall, the dog and cat lying in the pale yellow straw and the man in the dim basement room with the chipped iron bed, the broken leather sofa, and the table with the tasselled cover. They must have been listening for his footsteps, for the donkey brayed as the boy came up the mews and the dog and cat were on their feet when he opened the door to the building in which the stall was. Old Jock's voice croaked, "There you are," as Duggie came down the damp steps to the dustbins, which served the whole house, and the basement.

The man was sitting in an old-fashioned basket-chair by the gas fire. He was wearing his overcoat, which seemed unnecessary for the room was hot and stuffy. It looked too large for him; and without the usual cap, his face seemed grey and shrivelled. The cockiness and bravado had gone from the eyes and mouth. He seemed to have shrunken overnight into a smaller man.

"It's awful cold. Could you be buying me a little food while you're here?" he asked.

"Sure," Duggie nodded. He wanted to get out into the clear light of day, where people and things seemed healthier.

"There's a pound in the pocket of my coat hanging on the door. Could you get me a loaf and a wee bit of butter and a few eggs and something for the dog and cat. I've still got a wee drop of whisky and the milk-man will be calling, and there's plenty of tea in the tin."

Duggie took the money from the inside pocket of a grey jacket.

"Are you sure you don't want the doctor?" he asked.

"No, it's a chill I have, I'm thinking. I'm a strong

19

man yet and I'll not be wanting doctors for a while. Just a rest and plenty of warmth and to-morrow I'll be as right as the rain on Loch Mora on a September evening."

This romantic way of talking was a sign of sickness in the old man, Duggie decided as he went out to do the shopping.

As he fed the animals a little later he looked at the laden cart, at the sacks nearby filled with rags and at the odd pieces of iron piled in a corner. He remembered Old Jock saying it was time for him to pay a visit to the depot. Wonder if he would let me go instead, thought Duggie, imagining himself driving the donkey through London. He's probably getting short of cash.

"What about me taking the stuff, mister?" he asked presently, standing by the old man's chair.

"I would be grateful to you, but will you be safe? You have only driven the wee donkey with me beside you, and it will be a very different business all on your own."

"How far is the depot from here?"

"A few miles. They pay better the other side of the river. There are other places nearby, but I cannot agree with them. We fell out many years before."

"I expect I could find the way," said the boy, his heart warming to the idea.

"Get me a pencil and a piece of paper off the table by the window, and I will be drawing you a map to take you there. Do you think you will be lifting the iron and the sacks into the cart without difficulty?"

"Oh yes, I'm strong," Duggie said, doing as he was bade. "Can I take Toby?"

"Yes, the dog can go. He always does on that trip. Now here we are, lad, and this will be the road we took yesterday."

20

Presently Duggie was in the mews again, harnessing the donkey and loading the cart, being careful to see that too much of the junk was not at the back.

And then they were out on the road with the boy leading Tammy and the dog at his heels, and a clear sun breaking through the clouds and smoke of London, and casting gold across the dusty streets, and over the rooftops.

When the traffic was heavy the dog rode in the cart, standing proudly on the seat and barking at pedestrians, but Duggie walked all the way, not wishing to add his five stone to the donkey's load.

The fair fat man at the depot had wise eyes, like those of an owl, and bowed shoulders and an old peaked cap. And he wanted to know where Old Jock was.

"He isn't well. He's in bed, but he doesn't feel like seeing the doctor," Duggie said. "So I came along instead, seeing he needed the money."

"It's against the law. He can't employ little boys like you," said the man at the depot.

"I'm doing it for nothing. I like the donkey and it's my holidays and there's nothing else I want to do," said Duggie.

"You can't be more than eight. It isn't safe," said the man, pushing back his cap, so that a lock of fair hair tipped with grey escaped.

"I'm ten, nearly eleven. I haven't stolen the donkey or anything. I'm honest. Old Jock trusts me. He wouldn't have let me start out otherwise, would he?" Duggie wasn't annoyed; he knew grown-ups expected children of his sort to be dishonest. He was only anxious lest he should not get the money for the old man.

"I've got to buy a truss of hay for Tammy from

Welton's on my way back. Do you know where they are?" he finished.

"I meant you are too young to be allowed out in London with a donkey and cart. I can see you're truthful, because you don't mind looking me straight in the face. Besides you would never have found your way here if the old man hadn't told you and trusted you. Come on now, round through that door and we'll unload the cart and see how much we can give him this time." The man at the depot smiled for the first time as he finished speaking. His teeth were long and yellow, his fair moustache turned down a little at the corners as though it had been out in the rain too long.

They went to a yard and unloaded, and everything was weighed on scales or a large flat machine which seemed to have its works below ground.

"We'll make it five pounds ten, seeing he's ill, though by rights it shouldn't be more than five seven and sixpence," said the fair fat man.

He wrote out a receipt and Duggie signed it— Douglas Brown. Then he gave the boy the money in notes.

"And now I had better show you the way to Welton's, or the donkey will starve, I suppose," he said.

"I shall be able to drive Tammy now the cart's empty, right through London," said Duggie.

He wondered whether he ought to be a rag-and-bone man instead of a farm worker when he was grown up, but thinking of the lonely basement room, he decided not. Better a country cottage with the green windswept acres stretching to meet a clear smokeless horizon.

All the same he felt very happy sitting on the front of the cart with the reins in his hands, as Old Jock had shown him how to hold them, with Toby at his side, and London all around him, dirty, grey, mysterious, with people of all races and all creeds. He felt part of it as he crossed the Thames and saw the sun playing magic with the cold rippling water far below, and the tugs came up, and a hooter sounded, and a steamer belched smoke into the bright, brittle light of late December.

"Not long now before you're back in your stall, and we'll see how the old man is then," said Duggie, looking down at the grey back with the long black line running from wither to tail, and the great ears moving backwards and forwards with the gentle monotony of a clock's pendulum.

Chapter Four

"RAG AND BONES, rag and bones" . . . it was Duggie's voice this time and it didn't carry far. He had got Pete to come with him. "I won't be able to lift some of the stuff into the cart by myself," Duggie had explained, and Pete had obliged.

"It's better to ring the bells and ask. No one can hear you," said Pete now. "I'll stay with the donkey."

Duggie ran up the wide mosaic steps, and to the left of the door were six bells, each with a separate name in brass, above. . . . Jackson, Heal, MacIntyre, Hicks, Smith-Wrightson, Sharpe. . . . How was one to know which to ring? He decided on MacIntyre, because Jock had come from Scotland. There was no answer, so he tried Jackson and heard footsteps. He peeped through the letterbox and saw a light had gone on in the well-carpeted passage. The steps were those of a woman in high heels. They sounded brisk, certain, owned by a self-assured personality. Old Jock always said the rich were the least helpful. They couldn't be bothered to look out their old clothes or iron or papers. Duggie saw legs and shut the letterbox. They were slim legs in nylons, and this was an afternoon when most people were working. . . . Not much hope, Duggie thought.

The woman who opened the door had a dark, lively face, and a drawl to her voice, and she said, "Oh, what a darling donkey. Does he like carrots?"

Duggie said, "Have you any rags or bones, or old iron or paper, Madam? We give good prices." And the woman said, "But you are only little boys."

"The old rag-and-bone man is ill and we are helping him out. He's got no money," said Pete.

"Just newspapers would do," suggested Duggie, thinking there would be no old iron in this woman's flat.

"You've got nothing in the cart at all," she remarked now, screwing up her eyes because she was short sighted.

"We haven't been out long," lied Pete, not wishing her to know of their ill-luck so far.

"I've got an old coat of my husband's I was keeping for the next bazaar. You can have that, and I'll bring something for the donkey. Everyone else in the house is out I'm afraid," said the woman. "Has the old man seen a doctor? What about his old age pension?"

She went upstairs again without waiting for an answer and came back with a black coat, worn at the elbows and collar, and some carrots for Tammy and a biscuit for Toby, and a chocolate for each child, and presently the four of them were on the road again, feeling distinctly heartened. The next house gave them a bundle of old magazines, for which they paid three-pence, because the woman looked poor and seemed to expect something.

A man in a basement sold them a dressing-gown for a shilling. The next woman they brought to her door was grey-headed, bespectacled and disapproving. She asked them their names and addresses, and Duggie gave his, but Pete, more cunning, said he was John Smith of 6 Portobello Road.

She was grey-headed, bespectacled and disapproving

After that they were disheartened and went home, and Pete said he wouldn't come out with Duggie any more because he didn't like begging, and the clothes smelt. Duggie half-agreed, though he pointed out that they had paid for some of the things with the money Old Jock had given them. He didn't think it was much fun dealing with the rags and the paper, and no one seemed to have iron or bones. He wondered how the old man had stuck it for so long.

When they got back to the Mews they put Tammy into his stall and fed and watered him. Old Jock then appeared and said he was better, and he would feed the cat and the dog.

So Duggie went back to his house, and played with Freddie, who was fair and fat and six, and when his mother asked where he had been, he said out and about with Pete, and she was satisfied. He felt tired and happy and content in mind and body. But later in the evening there was a knock at the door and a tall policeman stood there when they opened it. And he said:

"Are you Mrs. Brown?"

She suspected Duggie at once, and turned to the boy and said, "What have you been up to?" and he said, "Nothing," and looked away.

The policeman came inside and he seemed to take up a great deal of room in the overcrowded kitchen. But when he took his helmet off, they could see he was young and nervous in spite of his size . . . "Only a boy really," Mrs. Brown said afterwards . . . and they were no longer frightened.

He explained that a woman had telephoned to say two boys by the name of John Smith and Douglas Brown were going round on behalf of a rag-and-bone man, and they were too young to be employed, and they should be stopped.

"It's not legal for a child under fifteen to work," the policeman explained.

"Never knew they were doing it . . . never," said Mrs. Brown. "There's a secretive little devil for you, never told me a thing."

"We weren't employed. We did it because the old man was ill and he needed money to feed the donkey.

26

But he's all right now. So we won't be going again. We didn't keep a penny for ourselves," said Duggie.

"We can't have kids going around begging rags and bones. It's not right. It's a disgrace to London," said the policeman. "I don't like old men doing it either, not anyone for that matter. But we can't stop it, not yet."

"You couldn't charge us for anything," said Duggie, who knew a boy who had been to a juvenile court and got off scot-free.

"Now what about John Smith? There's no one of that name at the address I was given. I suppose he gave a false one. Who was the boy with you, Douglas?"

Duggie didn't reply. He wasn't going to give Pete away and he didn't know what to say. He looked at the big wide face with the blue eyes which were set too high, and kept his own mouth shut.

"That'll be Peter Wright. But there's no point in you seeing him. I'll tell his mother. Duggie's the leader. Pete wouldn't have gone without him. Poor old Duggie's always been fond of animals. It's in his blood as you might say. He likes being with the donkey, and the cat and the dog, I expect," said Mrs. Brown.

"Did you know I was going there all the time?" asked the boy.

"I guessed that's where you were. But it's got to stop now," said his mother, getting slowly to her feet to pour boiling water on the tea leaves in the pot.

"Like a cup of char?" she asked the constable.

"No, thanks very much all the same. I must be getting along. Well, you won't be letting him go on the rounds again, then." The policeman put on his helmet.

"No, that's all right. He's a good boy really. Just wanted to help the old man. He's got a soft heart, our

Duggie has, the monkey. Sorry you've been bothered to come around. And you can trust me to have a word with Mrs. Wright."

"Very good, then. Good night. I'm glad to have it settled." The young policeman left, and for a few moments there was an uncomfortable silence.

"Don't you be doing that again," said Mrs. Brown at last. "Or you'll be getting us all into trouble, just when we don't want any. Besides it's not decent, a couple of kids selling rags and bones. They'll think I starves you. Gracious, I wonder whether anyone saw that bobby coming here. What will they all be saying? Still, you haven't committed any crime, I will say that. Just some busybody had to ring up the police because she had nothing better to do. Just ignorant. She ought to have three kids and another coming, then she might mind her own business."

"I'm awfully sorry, Mum, but Old Jock's better again now. I won't be going round with the cart again. Besides it was perishing awful, if you'd like to know, knocking at people's doors and having them looking at you like dirt and turning snooty," explained Duggie. "But I didn't think it was wrong. We wanted to help the old man."

"Maybe it isn't but it's got to stop. Get the cups out and we'll have a nice cup of tea, and that'll pull us together. Gracious, when I saw that great big policeman in the doorway I wondered what you *had* done. My heart was in my mouth, as you might say," said Mrs. Brown, sinking down on to Jennie's little bed which was in the far corner. And then suddenly she began to laugh, saying, "Oh my oh my," like an American, and then Duggie laughed, too, and they sat there rocking with their merriment, slopping their tea into their white saucers.

Chapter Five

SPRING HAD come to London: it was in the air, in the breezy March skies and in the sunlight which lay across the dusty streets in W.10. There wasn't much grass to be seen: only the tender blades at the edge of the play-ground and the buds on the plane trees spoke plainly of spring to Duggie Brown, catching the eye and crying out against the drab greyness, the dirty sameness of the area. Yet there was that feeling that something exciting was about to happen, some miraculous adventure lay in the future, round the corner. He felt it in his bones and went about with a sense of happy anticipation, which made him dreamy in the classroom and high-spirited out of school, like an overfresh horse.

"Mad as a March hare," his mother said, as he tore down the street on every one of the numerous errands on which she sent him.

Then one day the postcard came addressed to Master Duggie Brown. It said: *Dear Master Duggie, I am ill and may have to go into horspital and I'm afraid for the donkey. Will you be coming to see me soon? J. MacDonald.*

The Browns rarely received any post. Duggie's mother had read the card and discussed it with her husband before Duggie got back from school. Fred looked at it later and Mrs. Towers, their friend farther down the road, read it. They all knew it came from Old Jock.

"You had better go, seeing he's ill and all," said Mrs. Brown. "It's only Christian, as you might say."

Duggie was going anyway. He was feeling remorseful that he had not visited Old Jock and Tammy for over a month. Had the old man been ill and alone all that time? And who had fed the donkey, he wondered.

He went at once, found the hurricane lamp and a box of matches, and lit it. Tammy looked like the donkey in a picture in a biblical book, which Duggie had been given two years before by an elderly woman who wore fur tippets smelling of camphor and was said to be religious. In the flickering lamplight Tammy looked humble and little and meek. Duggie put his arms round the short straight neck and rubbed his face against the smooth coat.

There was plenty of hay on the donkey's stall, and presently Duggie walked up to the imposing row of houses and crept down the steps to Old Jock's room. He knocked on the door with his knuckles, but there was no reply and after a bit he noticed there was an envelope pinned above the knob. He took it out into the street under a lamp and saw his name was scrawled across it. Opening the envelope, he read: *Please look after Tammy. Exercise him every day if you can. He's rideable if you will not be wanting to bother with the cart. Toby and Flora are in my room. If my sister will not be taking them they will be put to sleep by the R.S.P.C.A. man. The ambulance is at the door. Enclosed please find two pounds. Spend it on the donkey. J. MacDonald.*

Duggie stood still for a long time. He felt very sorry for the old man and he wished he knew where he was. He wondered how he could find out and when the sister would come, and what she would be like. And then he went slowly back to the basement room and peered through the window and there were Toby and Flora sitting together on the leather sofa. He called their names and the cat started to mew pitifully, and he wondered when they had last been fed. Finally he drew the stub of a pencil out of a pocket and wrote on the back of Old Jock's letter: *Please don't have the cat and dog put to sleep, if you can't look after them. I'm sure I could find them each a nice home. I'm taking care of the donkey. Duggie Brown.*

He added his address at the bottom, scratched out his own name on the envelope and put *Old Jock's Sister* instead, and pinned it above the knob on the locked door to the basement.

Then he went back to Tammy, refilled the water bucket and inspected the hay and straw, finding there were two bales of the first and one of the second, which would last a donkey for three weeks, he thought.

He wished he could feed the dog and cat, but he didn't like to break into the basement room, and he hoped Old Jock had left them something.

He went straight home afterwards and told his mother the situation as she sat on a chair in the front doorway knitting a white vest for his baby brother or sister, which would be arriving soon. She took his news placidly, to his surprise, and made no objection to his assumption that he would now be seeing the donkey every day.

Duggie found his eyes straying from her plump handsome face to the grubby white ball of wool growing smaller and smaller every minute with the mechanical click of the needles. He didn't mind much whether the new baby was a boy or a girl, but he thought it would be nice for Jennie to have a sister. He didn't get on very well with his brother Fred, but he decided girls were different. Sisters always loved one another and when they reached their teens they went round arm in arm and confided in one another and giggled. A boy didn't really need a brother, Duggie thought, but girls needed sisters.

"Good thing the holidays will soon be starting if you ask me," said Mrs. Brown at last, watching her eldest son as he stood before her in the warm spring dusk. "Time I went indoors. Fancy me sitting out here all this time. Why, it's nearly dark. No one would think it was still March."

"It's our street lamp. Makes you forget night has come," the boy said. "It wasn't half dark down at Tammy's place, I had to take the notice to a light to read it. It's the dog and cat that I'm worried about. Could we have them, Mum, if no one else will? Seems all wrong that they should be destroyed. Toby's ever so clever. You should see him up in the cart, as proud as a king."

"What, us try to fit any more in this house? Don't know how we'll manage now, with another baby coming. You stick to looking after the donkey and that'll be quite enough." Her fat familiar hands collected the grubby ball.

"O.K., Mum. I'll carry the chair in for you. But perhaps I'll find someone else who would take them if the sister won't."

*   *   *

The next day the dog and cat had gone from the basement room, so he supposed Old Jock's sister had called for them.

He fed and watered the donkey and cleaned out the stall and left the manure where the men from the council could easily collect it. And then, when Tammy had digested, Duggie climbed on to his narrow back from an old crate and rode down the mews and out into the mean street and on into the murky depths of poorer London on a Saturday afternoon.

Grey light lay everywhere, no sun broke through the gloom of haze and smoke. People hurried with large shopping baskets, girls in tight-fitting trousers gazed with longing into shop windows or hung on the arms of dufflecoated men. Others teetered by, on high heels, wearing black-seamed stockings and skimpy suits, with bright vacant faces and gleaming hair. But Duggie was unaware of the passers-by; he knew only the swaying unsteady steps of the donkey carrying him, the clatter of the little hoofs on the tarmac, the firm body between his legs.

Without realising it he came down into the market, and here were stalls bright with vegetables and fruit, loud with orange carrots, green with lettuces and watercress, chicory and spring cabbage. Here were old clothes for sale, frocks drab and dusty as sacks, and new things shining with their newness, and stalls of old silver and plate, and saucers for a few pence, and old furniture looking lost and naked in the street.

Whistles greeted him. Youths called out comments. . . . "Ride 'em, cowboy" . . . "I had a donkey and it wouldn't go" . . . "On yer wye to the circus?"

Only jealousy, he thought. "Just ignorant," his mother would have said in the same circumstances.

He turned off into a quieter street, where a bunch of children were playing marbles in the gutter.

"Give us a ride," they said.

"Another day," Duggie told them. I must learn myself first, he thought.

He came to a fish-and-chip shop. Steam came in wisps on the grey air from a slot in the cloudy window, where customers put their hands to pay and take their purchases.

"Gee up, donkey. What are yer waiting for? Nuffink ter stop yer winning the Derby," shouted a darkly clad teddy boy lounging outside, a damp cigarette be-

"Ride 'em cowboy!

tween his lips and a practised nonchalance on the white pimply face beneath the forelock of waved hair.

But Duggie didn't care; he was happy on the donkey's back; he loved the narrow neck before him, the two dark lines which ran down behind the grey shoulders like a yoke, the long sad ears flapping to and fro with slow philosophical calm.

"You've got brains as well as sense, and I'm going to learn to ride you properly," Duggie said, patting the grey neck. "We're going to canter and gallop and everything. It will be a change after the cart!"

But who would help him? Could he learn all alone? He began to think of his friends. First his teachers at school. There was the red-haired one from Ireland; she was strict, but sometimes a smile of pure undiluted sympathy would cross her face when something awful happened to someone. It had happened to Duggie when an apple had fallen out of his pocket and rolled from end to end of the classroom during Arithmetic. And her smile had stopped the others laughing. But on other days she would hardly answer you when you spoke to her, and she might be like that when he asked about riding. There was Mrs. Towers, but she wouldn't know anything about donkeys. She had been in London all her life. And then there was the young woman at the library, who always asked after Fred and Jennifer when he went in, who never forgot their names. He saw her, a calm lithe figure climbing a little ladder to reach down a book, her grey eyes serious but kind, her small hands turning the white pages. She never minded how long he took choosing. She was interested in what he read. He would go there and try his luck. And she might be able to help with the dog and cat, too, for she was fond of books on animals and always recommending them to the children.

He turned now for home, up a wide road where gleaming painted houses looked through the green plane trees, and birds sang in back gardens, and poodles pranced on leads, and, urging the donkey forward, he trotted through the late March evening.

Chapter Six

"THERE'S NOT much demand for books on riding in this part of London you see, Duggie. I mean, none of your school friends ride, do they? In Kensington it's different. But I have got a couple of pony books. They're stories about children and ponies and one of them does include a few tips—sort of woven into the story. You could take those. They might help." The young librarian, whose name was Jane Howard, paused for a moment and Duggie felt the level grey eyes looking down on his own fair head. "What's it all about? Can I do anything, personally, I mean? I used to ride a lot when I was a kid. I competed in horse shows a bit too," she added, just as the silence was becoming unbearable to the boy.

"It's a donkey. I don't know if they are different to ride from horses," began Duggie, and then seeing Jane had sat down on a handy chair and relaxed, and the library was almost empty, he started to tell her the whole story, not forgetting the plight of Flora and Toby.

It seemed to the boy to take a long time, though the electric clock in the library had only progressed four minutes when he finished, and Jane's attention had never wavered for a second.

"Well, I can tell you how to sit on a horse, or rather a donkey—it's all the same—and how to make him increase or decrease his speed and that sort of thing. I'm no expert, but I know the elementary stuff," said the librarian.

"Oh, thank you, miss," began Duggie.

"You can call me Jane, if I'm going to help you a bit," she said. "Now what about stirrups?"

"What are those?"

"The things you put your feet in."

"I haven't a saddle. I ride straight on Tammy's back and he wears the driving bridle with blinkers," Duggie explained.

"Oh well, it's quite a good thing to start bare-back. Some cavalry schools used to make their men begin that way. One of the important things is never to be rougher than you need to be. Always try to stop the donkey with a lighter and lighter pressure on the reins, and make him go with a squeeze from the inside (not the back) of your calves rather than with a kick of the heels."

In between dealing with the children who came in for books, Jane told him what she knew about elementary riding, and then she told him to let her know if Toby and Flora were to be destroyed and she would see if she could find them a temporary home anywhere. Perhaps her mother, with whom she lived, might be able to help.

Duggie ran home as though there were springs on his feet, with two pony books under his arm.

"Miss Howard up at the library is going to help me," he told his mother and the two children, not being able to bring himself to call her Jane yet. "She's going to tell me how to ride better. She knows, you see. She used to jump in horse shows. And look, I've got these two books."

37

"Gracious, never seen anyone so excited. You quite gave me a turn, rushing in like that. Well, I'm glad you've got someone to help you, I must say. You deserves it, Duggie. I will say that," Mrs. Brown told him, reaching for the kettle. "Your Dad will be back in a few minutes. Have you made your bed now? You know you kids promised to help me a bit. And he's going to be strict on you."

"No, I was rushing off to ride Tammy and I forgot this morning, it being Saturday and all. I'll do it now, Mum. I'll read my books up there. It's too noisy down here, with Jennie and Dad and everything," said Duggie, his mind already stretching to the morrow when he would ride again, with knowledge of how it should be done.

The next day, which was Sunday, seemed a triumph because he learned to rise to the donkey's shuffling trot and to keep him closer to the side of the road—for Tammy liked to keep the same distance away from the kerb as when he pulled the little cart.

There seemed less people to jeer at Duggie's efforts and he knew they were lying late in bed. Many of those who were around were on their way to church or chapel and they smiled or nudged one another, rather than spoil their air of respectability with vocal comments. All over London the bells were ringing and they reminded Duggie that Easter would soon be here, as they sent their gay summons pealing through the grimy sunlit streets. He thought of the country in springtime, and when he saw the daffodils in the barrow on the corner of Edgerton Street he became nostalgic for something he knew only from two brief visits and the books he had read. He didn't see the mud at the farm gates, or the rain falling day after day on sodden fields. He saw only the romantic side and loved it passionately, faithfully, arguing with his schoolmates, who wanted only the faster and more brittle life of the town.

"Wouldn't you like to be sleeping out in a green field?" he asked Tammy as he bedded down the stall that night. "It's stuffy in here in the summer I should think. But I suppose you're used to it now, are you, little donkey, are you?"

He loved to spread the pale straw and to fill the low rack with sweet smelling meadow hay, while the old lamp sent forth its mellow light and shadows lay grey and changing on the floor. This new love was losing him his friend, Pete, but, looking back, he supposed they had been drifting apart for months. Pete's games held no charm for him now. He knew his heart was on riding and looking after this new and humbler friend.

He was ashamed how often in the next few days he forgot altogether about the old man languishing in hospital, as he rode in the early light of morning through deserted streets before going to school. The sister of Old Jock had left no notes about the dog and cat so far; every day he went to look on the basement door and was relieved to find nothing waiting for him.

Now his great wish was to canter, and yet his two pony books and Jane had made it clear that this must not be done on the roads. He asked a master at school where people cantered in London and he said Rotten Row, Wimbledon or Richmond. On the next Saturday morning Duggie started out towards Kensington in pale wintry sunshine with a light heart and a happy sense of anticipation. When he came to the High Street he remembered with a jolt that Old Jock was in hospital, and wondered whether he should enjoy himself so much in the circumstances. Here he became an object of interest and people began to point out the donkey and the boy to one another, and he was very aware of the endless hustling surge of

He suddenly let out a loud prolonged bray

traffic and the imposing hotels, and the smart prams and uniformed nannies on his left in Kensington Gardens.

He felt very low down on the little donkey and too close to the innumerable exhaust pipes belching smoke, but happier than he could ever remember being before. He saw the Prince Albert Memorial, the great Hall, and the Bowling Green which his school teacher had described to him. There were traffic lights and a road to cross and then the Row, brown and soft and dusty, with horses and ponies parading round like kings and queens.

Tammy's head came up two inches. He looked in

wonder and then suddenly let out a loud prolonged bray, which was echoed by the high old buildings and came back in mockery. For a few moments every ounce of energy seemed to have been drained from his body by the effort of producing that strange carrying sound, which ended in half-hiccup half-honk, then he leapt into action and bore Duggie across the peaty stretch as fast as his legs would carry him to the nearest group of horses. He stopped then as suddenly, beside a long-haired girl in a blue crash cap, black coat and cream breeches, riding a chestnut pony, who said, "Hallo, donk, what are you doing here?"

"Sorry," said Duggie, without thinking, staring at the tall man on a lovely grey on his right and a little girl on his left and then back at the smart long-haired girl in front of him. "I didn't mean to get in with your lot. He got excited all at once and brought me here."

"He's a good-looking donkey," said the man. "Anyone can ride in the Row, and lots of people run into trouble. Their ponies take off with them and that sort of thing, so don't worry. Does your animal jib? Lots of donkeys do."

"No, thank you, sir. He's very well behaved usually. I've never cantered before, so I brought him here to have a try, and he got excited when he saw you all. I reckon he gets bored by himself all the time."

"Well, come round with us, he'll go better then, and you'll see how we canter, not that we are so frightfully, frightfully good," said the smart girl.

"I've only been riding a week," Duggie admitted. "I wanted to get a proper book on it, a text one, but I couldn't. They haven't got one in our library."

"They ought to order one for you. They do sometimes at libraries. But I've got a beginner's one I never use now. I could lend it to you, if you like," said the

41

smart girl, as Duggie shortened his reins. "But it hasn't got a chapter on donkeys."

"How old are you, then?" asked the little girl, who had spectacles and was riding a grey pony and seemed to belong to the same group.

"Ten," said Duggie.

"Ten! But you're no bigger than me and I'm seven," she exclaimed, peering through her thick lenses.

"Don't be personal, Audrey," said the man.

"I might be a jockey if I don't grow too much," Duggie said.

"Well, come on, follow us, and we'll give you a gallop," the smart girl said.

All at once all the ponies and horses were cantering and Tammy was keeping up with them with surprising ease, and Duggie felt quite firm though he held on to the donkey's straggling mane with two fingers.

"He's jolly fast for a donkey," shouted the smart girl against the wind.

"The little thing's got quite a gallop," said the man. "Well stayed on, boy. Jolly good. Not bad for the first time."

They came to a standstill again, and all the ponies and horses wanted to talk to Tammy at once, as though congratulating him on his speed.

"He would win a Donkey Derby as easy as pie," said the girl in the crash cap. "You must enter him and begin your jockey career."

"But there isn't any Donkey Derby that I know of," said Duggie.

"Oh, yes, there is. In Sussex. *And a* Grand National, *and* 100 guineas, *and* racing in sulkies. I know, because I've been. There are proper bookies and everything."

"Blimey!" Duggie's mouth fell open. He could

42

think of nothing more to say. None of his wildest dreams had included a Donkey Derby.

"He's certainly got speed," said the tall man.

"Give me your address, and I'll send you that book. I think it's jolly sporting of you to bring a donkey to the Row." The girl's voice had condescension in it, and suddenly Duggie was aware of his rather ragged trousers, his ill-cut hair, and worn coat. These people looked so smart. How had he come to be with them? He felt small and untidy but he gave his address and thanked the girl, and then he tried to make the donkey leave for home, and he wouldn't, and Duggie hadn't a stick with which to support his legs because he had never needed one before.

"I had a donkey and it wouldn't go," a boy's voice chanted in the background.

"The little devil," murmured the girl in the crash cap.

"Never done it before," said Duggie, feeling his pale cheeks turn scarlet.

"We'll ride on," said the man on the big grey horse. "He'll probably be all right when we've all gone away."

The cavalcade left the donkey and the boy with a whirl of dust and the thud of hoofs on the brown track.

"Come on, Tammy, come on. There's a good little donkey," said Duggie, secretly deciding never to come to the Row again.

A taxi pulled up on the road; a mackintoshed figure with the chinless face of a rabbit and water-blue eyes jumped out.

"Wait a sec', sonny. I'd like to get a picture of you there. Hold it, there's a good boy," he said, whisking a camera from its case.

"I don't want no photographs ta̶̶̶̶," Duggie

implored, longing for Old Jock or the kind librarian to come out of nowhere and tell him what to do.

The camera clicked. The man said, "Just another," as though Duggie's words had never been uttered. The first spots of rain fell on the soft bare earth. The boy used his legs again and the donkey gave a little buck, and the man said, "Fine," as the camera clicked again, and the boy tipped forward on to the short thin neck.

"*He* won't win a Derby," laughed a passer-by, not aware for one moment that Duggie's mind had been on just that achievement. "Give me Brown Jack every time."

"Thanks," said the photographer, pushing the camera back into its case, jumping into the taxi, slamming the door and speeding away.

Now the boy was suddenly alone with the quiet spring trees, the young grass and the deserted track. A little farther on, he could see the Albert Memorial and Hall and the procession of buses and traffic. In those brief seconds of solitude Tammy and Duggie relaxed; calmness came, and the next moment the donkey was walking on with his head set for home, as though nothing in the world could disturb him.

Chapter Seven

"WELL, I never! Fancy our Duggie getting his picture in the paper. Why they didn't mention his name, I can't think," said Mrs. Brown, looking at the London *Evening Despatch* for the fourth time. "A young rider in the Row this afternoon," she read again. "Gracious, what will the nipper be doing next, I'd like to know?"

Her brown eyes sparkled with pleasure. Duggie knew she would never disapprove of his being with the donkey now. By mere chance he had won her approbation. "You don't half look sheepish," she said.

"I felt it, too. Tammy wouldn't go," he told her and the wonderful adventure of the morning came back to him in full. "I galloped him. I kept up with the horses, though they only cantered of course. The man said he was fast for a donkey, ever so fast." He paused and decided not to mention the Donkey Derby. That would be a secret between Jane and himself, and, perhaps, the girl in the blue crash cap if she sent him the textbook. Now he had galloped once he wanted to do it again, and yet it was a long way to take Tammy to the Row, and he felt a little self-conscious riding a donkey amongst the horses and the properly dressed riders. All evening he thought about the problem, and at night while he slept his mind must have worked for he wakened with a solution. There was the old bombed site half a mile away. Once four terrace houses had stood there, with white porticos, and gleaming steps. Then after a raid in 1943 there had been craters and broken masonry, bits of walls, a window gaping like a mouth without teeth. A few months ago the site had been cleared and levelled; in one half some foundations had been laid, and then suddenly, inexplicably as far as Duggie was concerned, the work had stopped. The bricklayers had gone away, grass had broken through the brown earth, and the indomitable willow herb had begun to show green here and there.

Duggie saw that site now as his schooling ground. He would mark out a school with bricks, like a character in one of the pony books he had from the library, and he would train the donkey to obey his aids. He could canter there to his heart's content. He sang as he helped his mother get breakfast that morning, and she thought the photograph had raised his spirits. "Don't you be getting too big for your boots," she said, taking a comb off the cooker to do Jennie's hair.

On the door to the donkey's stall there was a notice when he got there. It said: *Can't keep the dog and cat any longer. My landlord won't have it. I've told Jock. If you know anyone who would have them I should be obliged. Mrs. E. Tinsel, 3 Prater Road, W.3.*

He didn't know whether Jane would be at the library in the morning. He decided to see her in the afternoon, and he rode Tammy to the bombed site, and spent an hour there, and at the end of that time he was very stiff, but much firmer on the donkey's back, and he and the little grey animal were beginning to understand each other very well indeed. As he rode back down sunlit streets, and heard birds singing in the plane trees, he thought again of the dog and cat and immediately after lunch he hurried to the library.

"I live with my mother. It's our house, so I don't have to bother about landladies. I'll have them for a bit. You collect them and bring them here at seven to-morrow night. Borrow a hamper for the cat," said Jane, and her small thin hands continued to sort the books as she spoke. "How are you getting on with your riding?" she asked after a bit. And then Duggie told her all about the Donkey Derby, and about his gallop in the Row, and Jane said, "Jolly good. Luck to you," and his happiness seemed to grow with every word she spoke, and he forgot the old man in the hospital bed, and the donkey seemed to be his own property. He whistled all the way home. The street was becoming used to Duggie's whistling. In the evening he managed to borrow a hamper from the woman at the newsagent's, so next morning he went in search of Mrs. Tinsel.

She seemed thin and creepy like a spider when he found her. The cat and dog welcomed him as an old friend, and he felt they had not been happy in her stuffy little bed sitting-room. She told him Jock was progressing well, and would be out soon. He never thought of asking what the old man was suffering from, and it was something he never knew.

He was glad to leave Prater Road with the cat in the hamper and the dog on a lead and a London wind blowing his hair, so that it stood on end like wheat straw off a combine. He locked Flora and Toby in Tammy's stall while he rode the donkey on the bombed site during the afternoon, and bought meat for them with Old Jock's money on his way back.

Jane gave exclamations of joy when she saw them. "My mother will just love the cat. And we haven't had a dog for years," she said and, walking home, Duggie felt very adult. He had dealt with all the old man's animals now, and everything would be all right when Jock came out of hospital.

The next day he had his first fall. The donkey jibbed suddenly and Duggie went over his head. He had a bruise the size of an egg, where his scalp had met a stone. He combed his hair carefully and his mother never noticed it. Things were moving fast. When he got home at dusk he found a parcel awaiting him. It was the book on riding sent by the girl who had ridden in the park in a blue crash cap. She signed herself Joan Worthington-Smith, and she also enclosed some details of a Donkey Derby to be held fifty miles out of London on Whit Monday. The biggest event at this meeting had a first prize of a hundred guineas, and the entry fee was ten pounds. The prize dazzled Duggie but he was daunted by the thought of raising the entry fee. Ten pounds seemed an impossible amount of money to him as he stood in

47

the overcrowded little kitchen, with the smell of onions in his nose and the blare of the wireless in his ears.

"I don't want noffink to eat ternight," whined Freddie.

"Now then, speak nice or you'll never get anything any more . . . noffink!" scolded Mrs. Brown, arms akimbo, by the stove. The fat spitting in the frying-pan competed now with the B.B.C. Suddenly, for no reason it seemed, Jennie started to cry. Duggie went to her, speaking softly as he spoke to Tammy. When she had quietened he retreated to the little room upstairs to lie on his black iron bed and horsehair mattress, and read the book on riding. There were twenty diagrams, as well as some instructive photographs and he soon realised he had been holding the reins in the wrong way.

By ten o'clock next morning he was putting into

"Leave him alone or I'll throttle the life out of you!"

48

practice all that he had learned from the book. It seemed to Duggie that Tammy went better than ever before. He forgot he was on a donkey with a shuffling gait, and thought of his little mount as the most handsome steed in the world, gifted with handiness and speed. He was mad to progress; being able to sit bareback at the gallop was not enough. He decided, on the spur of the moment, to learn to jump. In a corner was a pile of bricks. He tied the donkey to a post at the roadside, and started to build a low wall in the middle of the site. About ten inches high will be enough to start with he thought, sweating back and forth with a brick in each hand. He was completely absorbed when he heard a jeering cry, followed by a shout of "That'll make 'im run!" And he looked up to see three lanky boys with a strange akinness to one an-

other, though their sizes differed, stoning the donkey.

By nature he was not quick-tempered, but now his mouth uttered words over which he seemed to have no control.

"Leave him alone or I'll throttle the life out of you. Stop that! Do you hear? Get away. Put down that stone. I'll knock you down!" As these words poured forth his legs bore him across the site, his eyes afire, his hands, a brick in each, gesticulating furiously, his hair pale as raffia. Sense came to him just in time; he dropped the bricks almost at the same moment as his hands came up to hurl them at two of those three dark heads.

"Don't you dare touch my donkey again," he said in a calmer voice.

"'Ark at 'im. Do you 'ear? Lord Muck if you like. Go on, Frankie, give the donkey one with the stick. Turn 'im loose," said the tallest boy, whose cheeks seemed the sallowest.

The urchin called Frankie raised a stick and brought it down behind Tammy's ears. "'It 'im on the ear'ole!" he shouted with bestial triumph in his voice. The third boy started to unhitch the donkey's reins. "We'll make 'im run," he laughed, his cheeks suddenly two wide blobs of colour.

"I'll get the R.S.P.C.A.," threatened Duggie, and then when the stick came down again, across the dark lines which made a yoke on Tammy's shoulders, something in Duggie's brain snapped. He hurled himself through space. His hands groped wildly for Frankie's face. It was pale as paper; the hair like a mop of dark seaweed, the neck scrawny with a bulging Adam's apple. "I'll kill you," said Duggie's voice, hoarse and unfamiliar with hate, but the boy's knee came up and dug him in the stomach. His hands never reached the jeering face. For a second he doubled up

50

with pain and then he straightened himself, and his right fist shot out for Frankie's jaw.

There was a yell of pain as knuckles met the hard bone, and then he felt hands on his shoulders, longer fingers, gripping and pulling him backwards. Behind and above he saw in sudden terror the sallow face, the gaunt cheeks, and narrow eyes of the tallest boy.

"Three against one. Not fair!" he gasped, as his body overbalanced and he went back, back and then landed on earth sprinkled with a few tender blades of grass. The boy's weight was on top of him, now hands pinioned his arms. He felt his terror evaporating, his brain beginning to work again. "Let me get up," he said, and his voice was clear and steady, though his heartbeats were as loud as a drum.

"Now, who's going to do the throttling?" asked the wide mouth four inches above Duggie's face, while the fingers tightened, pinching his arms, digging through his coat into his flesh. "Tell me that."

"Three against one, and you're all bigger than me," said Duggie and he tried to look his captor straight in the eyes.

"Cocky, ain't 'ee," said the boy who wasn't Frankie. "Beat 'im up, George. Teach 'im a lesson."

Frankie suddenly advanced, stick raised, and clouted him twice across the legs. "That'll teach yer to go 'itting one of the Smithson gang," he said.

He felt his fear coming back then. He was utterly in their power. He looked at the three gloating faces, at the six eyes bright with speculation. He prayed that Jane might come, his mother or a friend. A knot tightened in his throat: the disgraceful shameful tears rose to his eyes.

"Look at 'im! Cry baby!" jeered Frankie and dirty teeth showed with his smile.

"We'll teach you to go interfering with us. No one

51

challenges the Smithson gang and gets away with it, see?" said George, and Duggie noticed he spoke better than the others.

"What are we going to do wiv' 'im?" asked the third boy. "Let 'im off wiv' a beating?"

It seemed to be up to George to make the decision.

"Make 'im say 'e's sorry," said Frankie. "Make 'im say 'e'll never challenge us again."

"Come on, kid, say it," said George.

"You hit my donkey," said Duggie with stubbornness in his voice.

Frankie lit the dog-end of a cigarette. "Burn 'is cheek wiv' that," he said, with an ugly leer too old for his years.

"You don't want that to happen, do you?" asked George. "Come on, say you are sorry you hit Frankie." His voice was suddenly kinder.

"But I'm not," said Duggie.

"I'll kick yer. I'll kick yer perishin' teeth in," said Frankie," "and your donkey's too."

"I'm not afraid. You can kill me if you like. Then you'll be hanged," said Duggie and he tried to sound scornful. "Three against one on the donkey, and now three against one on me. That's not much of a gang. Let me get up and have a square fight with one of you."

The three boys looked at one another. It seemed an anti-climax. They had stopped to stone the donkey as they stoned many animals, without thinking, without cause. If anyone asked them why they had done it they wouldn't have known how to answer. Now they didn't know what to do.

" 'Ere you are. Git 'im to say 'e's sorry wiv' that," said Frankie at last holding the smouldering dog-end out to George. " 'E ain't going to go till 'e's apologised for 'itting me on the mouf."

But Duggie knew, and they all knew, that the heat of the moment was over. Only Frankie was still revengeful. George's fingers no longer pinched in anger, and Duggie's tears had petered out.

"Garn," said George. " 'E's only a little 'un. Can't be more than eight or nine."

"I'm ten," said Duggie unwisely.

And then suddenly in this moment of indecision things began to happen. First of all the donkey let out a loud and hideous bray, which made the Smithson gang nearly jump out of their dingy shoes. Then a car drew up and a man in a Homburg jumped out and said, "What are you doing to that little boy?" And an elderly woman with an umbrella appeared from nowhere, and said, "I've been watching them from a window. They stoned his donkey." Duggie was suddenly afraid that someone might call a policeman. "It's all right," he said. "It was a bit of a mistake."

"Get off that boy. Do you hear what I say?" The man in the Homburg had a face like an angry rat's.

"Bully," said the woman with the umbrella, brandishing it like a weapon.

"We haven't hurt him. Haven't hit him once, as it happens. And look what he did to Frankie's chin. Look at the bruise coming out of it." George got to his feet as he spoke.

"He's a brave little chap. He protected a dumb animal," said the woman.

"I want your names and addresses," said the man, bringing out a tattered notebook and a ballpoint pen.

"O.K., Jack, Frank and Peter Silver, 13 Grove Crescent, W." answered George and the words came out so pat that Duggie knew they were false. The man seemed satisfied, however, though he didn't say whether he intended going to the police. "We'll just

53

see the little boy safely on his way with the donkey," he said to one one in particular.

"Come on. Get going," hissed George, and the next second the Smithson gang had taken to their heels. "Good riddance," said the man.

"What a dear little donkey. What do you feed him on?" asked the woman, tucking her black umbrella under her arm.

"Hay and a bit of corn," said Duggie, going across to Tammy.

"No grass?"

"No, 'fraid not." He was tired of the whole affair. He wanted to get away.

"Well, if ever he needs a little nibble my garden's over there, No. 8 Charles Crescent. There's some rough stuff round the trees which needs keeping down. Bring him in any time."

"Thanks," said Duggie, vaulting on to the grey back, seeing happily the familiar ears before him, feeling suddenly divorced from all which had happened in the last ten minutes.

"They've made off. You'll be all right now," said the man in the Homburg, tucking away his notebook, getting into his car.

"Just took their names to frighten 'em," he said as he closed the door. "Nothing like paper and pencil to frighten some rough youngsters."

Tired, with all thought of jumping abandoned for the day, Duggie turned for home, climbing slowly the long steep dusty incline which led to poorer, narrower streets. To-morrow, he thought, I must decide how to raise ten pounds. I haven't written to the girl who sent the book yet. Goodness, what a long name she has—wouldn't like it myself, too much of a mouthful. Somewhere a church clock chimed out the noontide. Reaching the top of the hill, Duggie pushed the little donkey into a trot. He wasn't going to think about those boys till later. He had to do some sorting out in his mind. They had come suddenly out of the blue and he was afraid. They would come again.

Chapter Eight

IT WAS two days later when he suddenly thought of the woman with the umbrella in connection with the ten pounds. He had already approached Jane, and she had seemed without ideas, so that he supposed she was hard up herself. But the woman, Duggie told himself, had looked the type to have a pretty penny in the bank. She most likely had much more than she needed, doing nothing at all but bring in a few pence a year. She might not mind backing him and Tammy in the Donkey Derby, if it meant a chance of winning a hundred guineas. And if she lost a tenner it wouldn't seem very much to a single woman with a large house and a garden with grass round the trees.

To-day he started to teach the donkey to jump, while keeping an ear open for the Smithson gang, whom he dreaded—for they seemed half-mad to him, and unpredictable. He fell off once when Tammy refused, and had two fights with the donkey, who, suddenly bewildered, refused to go forward or move in any direction for ten minutes on end. But, on the whole, Tammy seemed the least stubborn of animals, and Duggie supposed this was because Old Jock had always treated him well, but firmly—never asking him to take too heavy a load or go too far in a day.

By eleven o'clock Tammy had jumped a wall of one foot three inches in height, and the boy decided to head for Charles Crescent and try his luck there. No. 8 was a tall house with a stucco façade and Georgian windows. There were shrubs in the little bit of garden in the front, which seemed in keeping with the owner's appearance and temperament. There were several bells by the door, and Duggie realised with a pang that she must have let some of the rooms; perhaps that meant she wasn't so rich after all. He rang the largest press-button and waited. Tammy stood patiently; he was used to waiting. He was very humble and looked especially so against this high house.

An age seemed to pass before Duggie heard footsteps, and then he supposed a uniformed maid was coming to the door, for he could not believe anyone who was not rich would live there. But it was the woman herself who opened it, and she wore an apron, and, now that she was not puffed out with anger, her cheeks seemed more hollow and her body thinner than when he had last seen her. Thick blue veins stood out on the backs of her work-worn hands, her shoes were black and laced; her stockings thick lisle. Her beige jumper had a dirty mark where it met her long neck.

"So you *have* come. I am glad. I didn't think you would. And oh, isn't it a dear little donkey? So patient and understanding." She spoke in a thin, almost querulous voice.

She wasn't as Duggie remembered her. She wore spectacles now; old-fashioned tortoiseshell ones. He couldn't imagine her lending him ten pounds. She probably disapproved of gambling.

"I'll just take you round to the back and show you the grass," she said, surprised by his silence. Her legs were like sticks, he thought, as he followed her through the split-oak gate.

"I thought you were so plucky the other day," she said.

56

He couldn't think of any reply.

"Never met them before," he muttered at last.

"And I hope you never will again," she said. "Here you are. Supposing you tie the donkey to the tree and

He sat very stiffly on the edge

then come inside while he grazes and have a cup of tea or a glass of milk, whichever you prefer, with me." Her eyes were smiling kindly with her mouth, as she spoke, and he felt hope again.

"Thank you very much," he said, taking the bit out of Tammy's mouth, making the pair of reins into one, which he then tied to the noseband at one end and to the tree at the other.

The rooms inside the house seemed very large and high. He was told to sit down in an arm-chair, upholstered in dark red with an antimacassar. He sat very stiffly on the edge. There were a great many photographs; wedding groups, young men with huge moustaches, girls with bandeaux round their heads, and an army officer on a Roman-nosed charger. There were several lamps set here and there on some of the numerous little tables, and a writing-desk with over-flowing pigeon holes, and rugs on the parquet floor, and a great sofa with tassels. The woman brought him a glass of milk and biscuits. He wished she had brought something for herself too. He felt silly eating and drinking by himself.

"How long have you had the donkey?" she asked, as he bit into the first biscuit.

"He's not mine. Owner's in hospital. I'm looking after him."

Gradually she got the whole story out of Duggie, even his hopes of competing in the Donkey Derby. She didn't offer to lend him ten pounds. He was very conscious of the crumbs he had allowed to fall on the carpet.

"He's very fast for a donkey, you see," the boy said for the third time.

"Ten pounds is a lot to risk, and you don't know how fast the other donkeys will be. You haven't tried him against one, have you? Couldn't you just enter him for the races which have smaller prizes and entry fees?" asked the woman, picking up the empty glass and plate. "No, don't move, stay where you are. I can manage."

"I sort of set my heart on the big race. I've got a kind of feeling about it," said Duggie, sitting down again.

She went out and came back. "Well, I'm afraid I can't lend you the ten pounds. I have to let three-quarters of this house to make ends meet. And I've got to have the decorators in to do the kitchen. You see, you may never be able to pay it back," she said. And now that she knew what the boy was after Duggie felt ashamed of his request and of the way he had hinted about it, instead of coming straight to the point if he was going to ask at all.

"Now do you think you ought to pop outside and see how the donkey is?" she suggested. "I could *give* you a pound for one of the other races."

"Oh, I couldn't take that," said Duggie, blushing. "Thank you very much. I couldn't accept gifts of money. If someone backed Tammy by putting in the ten pounds, they would stand a chance of winning a hundred. It wouldn't be a loan really, but a sort of bet." He realised now that he had approached the whole matter in the wrong way.

But she wasn't impressed by the argument. She was walking to the front door, with one hand stretched out to pull back the latch. No hope here, he thought, no hope anywhere, probably.

Tammy was still grazing busily when they got outside and they watched him in silence for a bit before Duggie mounted and rode away, after thanking his hostess for her hospitality to them both. She was a nice old thing really.

He remembered there was still plenty of time in which to make his entry for the big race, and he toyed with the idea of running a raffle, but he thought that would most likely be wrong. One could only do it in aid of some charity, he decided.

He turned the last corner before the mews and felt a sharp blow on the head; a stone fell to the ground. It must have come from a catapult. He looked round and saw nothing, but heard running feet down a side road. The Smithson gang, he thought, and he urged Tammy into a trot. He supposed he might consult

Jane about these enemies which had come into his life with so little warning or provocation, and about the ten pounds too.

Ten minutes later when he was brushing the donkey in the stall, he heard a familiar voice behind him.

"So you've exercised him already this morning. You will be making a fine rider, I'm thinking."

Out on the grey cobbles in the mews stood Jock, a pale ghost of what he had been. Duggie stared at him dumbfounded.

"Didn't expect me back so soon. You would not be expecting me yet. Och, I am finished with the doctors. I would like you to know you've been looking after the donkey very well. I'm right pleased with you, lad," said Old Jock.

Duggie came out of the stall and said, "I'm ever so glad to see you back. Are you quite well now? You know where the dog and cat are?"

Fancy me fussing so much about the ten pounds, and forgetting Old Jock would come back and take the donkey on the rounds again any day, he thought.

"You sound awful flat. I shall not be using the wee donkey in the cart for a wee while, I'm thinking. So you will not be missing your riding all at once. The man in the garage told me how you've been setting out every morning."

"No, I'll stop now you're back. You will want to earn some money. I've nearly finished the two pounds. I got a new truss of hay delivered yesterday, and I had to spend some money on feeding the dog and cat when I had them here."

"There's no want about it. I will not be strong enough for a few days, and I will be glad if the donkey would be having a wee bit of exercise. He will be getting bored standing by himself in that stall all day."

Duggie burst out suddenly, "Would you like to win

a hundred pounds, would you?"

Then, sitting down in the pale straw, he started to tell Old Jock about his ride in the Row, about the photograph in the paper, about Joan Worthington-Smith and the Donkey Derby.

When he had finished Old Jock said, "I will not be living much longer. They say in the hospital that I made a fine recovery, but I have my doubts. So what is ten pounds out of the money I put by? Och, it will not be missed, I'm thinking. You take it, lad, and enter the donkey and if he will not be winning it will not be of great account. If I live long enough I will be selling Tammy for a tenner. I cannot see myself on the roads again. We will be keeping the donkey till after Whitsun and who knows what the good Lord will see fit to give us."

Duggie thought hospital had changed the man, made him more tolerant; he seemed to be accepting his bad health as he had not done before. In a way it was pathetic.

"I'll try to win it. I'll do my best. Gosh, if you could have a hundred guineas!" said the boy, looking with sorrow at the furrowed face, the pale lips and the white hands, and thinking: then he could move out of that room into somewhere airy and light.

"We will be splitting it half and half. That will be the fairest way. I will back the donkey with five pounds and will be lending you the other five pounds. That's the way it will be working, lad."

Talking had tired the old man. He looked like a scarecrow now, Duggie thought, too small for his herringbone tweed coat . . . a figure to be lain flat by the smallest gust of wind . . . a bent reed . . . a broken man.

"I should go inside," the boy said. "Shall I make you a cup of tea? You ought to keep warm." He was haunted by remorse for having thought so little about Old Jock while he lay sick in hospital, and alarmed now by his appearance.

"No, I can manage, thank you."

"Sure?"

"Sure, thank you."

As he walked home he realised he liked Old Jock, but he had never missed him, as he would have missed the donkey. The possiblity of winning fifty guineas did not occupy Duggie's mind at all. He thought mostly of the excitement of riding in the race, and as he turned up his own narrow street he wondered how the entries would be started—by gun or flag or tape?

Chapter Nine

HE THOUGHT suddenly of the Smithsons as he opened the door to his parents' rooms. Would they turn up again to mar an almost cloudless sky?

His mother was sitting heavily on a cane-seated chair by the cooker.

"Here you are at last. Thought you were never coming. I've got a bit of a pain in me back to-night. You'd better get the supper. The others have had their tea. You had better eat with Dad, seeing you're so late. He'll be in presently. There's a nice bit of plaice on the table," she said, and the tone of her voice wasn't quite as usual.

Suddenly the Donkey Derby was forgotten. The Smithsons were wiped from the boy's mind like chalk from a blackboard. And he looked at his mother's pale face and thought only of the baby which was to be born to the Browns this week. Had the moment come? And what was he to do? He was overwhelmed with a sense of helplessness and ignorance. But he kept his voice calm.

"What about you, Mum? You'll manage a little bit of fish, won't you?"

"No, I couldn't face anything just now, thanks. You can give Dad my piece. He needs plenty."

Her voice was completely normal now, and he began to wonder whether it would be a boy or a girl, when it did come.

"Nothing to worry about, Duggie. I think I'll have a lie down all the same," said Mrs. Brown, and she went into the room behind the kitchen.

We'll *have* to have a council flat. They can't refuse to accept the next we're offered if we have another baby in the family, the boy thought. "Would you like me to make you a cup of tea?" he called, peering into the bedroom a few minutes later.

"No, thanks, love. Tell Freddie to go to bed, will you? And then pop down and fetch Mrs. Towers and don't loiter on the way, mind."

"And what about the fish?" Duggie had taken trouble with his cooking.

"Leave it, switch off the stove. Or put it in the oven, turned low. I don't mind. But get Fred off to bed and fetch Mrs. Towers."

She lay down again and added, "All right, nothing to worry about, but don't be long, now."

Duggie pulled his reluctant brother upstairs and watched him undress in the room they shared. Jennifer was already asleep in the kitchen. No normal noise wakened her.

He could just remember his mother going off in the middle of the afternoon before his sister was born. "To see the stork," Mrs. Towers had said.

Now he was running down the narrow street, be-

tween the low houses empty of ornament. Hunger
came suddenly; his tummy gnawed; and his feet clattered, the only feet in view. All around the April air
was warm and full of hope. Lights gave out a gentle
glow through open windows and the smell of frying
permeated the spring night, and hung about the street
increasing his hunger.

Mrs. Towers was at her sink. Her hair hung in grey
rats' tails, but her smile was warm and welcoming. Her
big arm went on Duggie's shoulders.

"And you're worried, lovey, aren't you? It don't
take a wizard to see that. But there's nothing to bother
your head about. Just let me change me shoes and
take off me apron and I'll be along there. I've been
expecting her to send you along these last three evenings. Dad's not at home, I suppose?"

"No," said Duggie. "Mrs. Towers, will the baby be
born soon?"

" 'Spect you'll have a little brother or sister by
morning. It's just right, not early nor late, on the day.
Perfect," she said, straightening her hair before the
cracked looking-glass which hung above the sink.

"Righto, love, off we go. And don't be scared like.
You was born once yourself, weren't you?" She
smiled at him as though they were in some joint con-
spiracy, and he felt her pleasure and excitement.

"She looked all right," he said. "She told me not to
worry."

Walking with this big woman, his fears were subsid-
ing. She knew it all, and he knew nothing. Her com-
petence and self-assurance were like an armour against
worry for him.

"Had three myself, you see, lovey. So I do know
something about it," she explained. "Cor, won't your
dad be thrilled. Wonder if it will be a boy or a girl?
Which does she want?"

"I don't know."

"Aren't you excited? Goodness, when my little sister was born I was that thrilled! Oh, she was a dear little thing, pretty as a picture. Auburn her hair was, just five strands of it, and her eyes were as blue as the sky, lovely, she was."

"I would like a girl for Jennifer," Duggie said. "I want it to be called Rosemary. I've thought about that quite a bit."

"I bet you have. And I bet it won't be so long before you're a man yourself with a wife, and a kid of your own coming. You'll see."

Duggie couldn't picture it, but he supposed she was right. She seemed to know so much, to be so self-confident. Sometimes he almost wished she was his mother and then afterwards he was ashamed.

"I'm going to ride Old Jock's donkey in the Derby," he said suddenly, wanting to confide in someone.

"You've got hopes," she said, laughing and then, seeing his downcast face, "It's a fine ambition and the old man appreciates what you've done for him, really he does, so I'm told."

Now they had arrived and Mrs. Towers disappeared into the back room. Duggie took the plaice out of the frying-pan, where the fat had congealed, and put them in the oven on a tin plate. In his anxiety he forgot to light the oven, but he didn't find that out till afterwards. Jennie was asleep, her golden hair spread on the pillow, her long light lashes meeting to make one thick flaxen fringe. Duggie hoped again that the new baby could be Rosemary, and he saw it with golden hair too and bright cheeks. Now he had dealt with the fish he didn't know what to do. He stood by the window and watched a black and white mongrel with a curly tail set out alone for a walk. The dog's air was very purposeful and Duggie wondered where he was

65

going, and then he began to wonder how soon Old Jock would want Flora and Toby again and he wondered too whether one day Jane would marry and have a baby.

Mrs. Towers came out of the room then. "Her time has come," she announced in momentous tones, and her blue eyes stared importantly into Duggie's pale face. But he didn't speak, because he didn't know what to say, and then Mrs. Towers's tone became more practical. "She says she wants a taxi. I don't want to leave her just now. Do you think you could get one, love?"

"Righto," said Duggie, making for the door, pleased to be doing something to relieve his own tension. He ran up the street again to a bigger brighter road, and then his eyes began their quest for a taxi for hire. At first they all seemed occupied by passengers apart from one, the driver of which said he had finished for the day. As minutes passed in failure Duggie began to panic. He thought of the two women at home waiting, expecting to see him every second, to hear the click of a taxi meter at the door. If only Dad hadn't been late back, he thought, straining his eyes to the farthest point to which they were capable of seeing. Another taxi came, and he waved wildly only to see its *for hire* sign was down. He decided to run up to the crossroads. At the top he saw Frankie, who called, "Hallo, donkey boy," and pulled a catapult out of his pocket, and then seeing so many people around put it out of sight hastily. "Wot's the 'urry?" he asked.

"Mum's having a baby, I've got to get a taxi," shouted Duggie, glad to have anyone to whom he could communicate his important and so far fruitless mission.

"Well there's one. Cab, cab," yelled a young man with a rolled umbrella. "No good, it's full, blast it."

66

"Can't get nothing," said Duggie. "And she's waiting with Mrs. Towers."

"I'll see what I can do. They are more likely to

Duggie began to panic

stop for me," said the young man, looking at Duggie's worn jacket and grey shorts.

They stood together for a moment, searching in vain the steady procession of cars for an empty taxi. Then the young man said, "I'll tell you what, I'll slip in the pub here and ring the rank round by my place. It's only a few hundred yards from here and I've got the number in my diary. Just wait a moment, and I'll be back."

He disappeared into the public bar of a pub, which Duggie hadn't noticed before, and came back a minute or two later smiling. "That's all right. One will be here any second now. I'll stay to see everything is all right. Do you know where it is to go?"

"To hospital," said Duggie.

"Yes, but to which, which part of London?"

"Oh, I dunno. They didn't say," said Duggie, feeling incompetent.

"Never mind. I expect they were in too much of a flat spin. Here it is." He waved his umbrella and the taxi drew majestically to a standstill.

"This boy's mother has got to go to hospital. It's urgent, going to have a baby," the young man started to explain to the driver.

"Where we got to go?" asked the driver.

"Five Stroughton Street," said Duggie.

"Which maternity hospital, St. Mary's?"

"The boy doesn't know. He'll go with you to Stroughton Street, and they'll tell you then. Get in, and tell him the way to your mother's place, if he doesn't know it," said the young man to Duggie.

The boy had never been in a taxi before. He liked the shiny seat, the smell of leather, but his mind was agitated.

"I know Stroughton Street," said the taxi driver, putting down the meter.

"Good-bye, good luck. She'll be all right," said the young man.

"Good-bye. Thank you, sir," shouted Duggie, remembering his manners as the taxi drove off.

"I 'spect it's St. Mary's. Most of them round 'ere goes there," said the driver.

"I dunno. She wanted to go by taxi," said Duggie, thinking how nice the young man had been and hoping with all his heart that Mr. Brown would have returned by the time the taxi reached Stroughton Street. But he hadn't and Mrs. Towers's face had lost much of its composure.

"Thank the lord you're here at last, Duggie. We'd done better to have telephoned," she said.

"I couldn't help it," the boy said and he glanced at the clock and saw he had in fact only been away twelve minutes in all, though it had seemed an age to the two women and himself.

"St. Mary's?" asked the taxi driver, as Mrs. Brown clambered inside, looking, Duggie thought, rather white and strained.

"The maternity wing. Now don't you worry, Duggie. I know she looks bad just now. But it will be all over very soon. There's nothing on earth to worry about. By morning you'll have a lovely baby brother or sister," said Mrs. Towers.

Mrs. Brown managed to smile. "Tell Dad what's happened. I expect he'll come round to the hospital. Tell him it's right to the day. Look after yourself and the others, Dug, and don't forget to give your Dad those two pieces of plaice." The smile lit up her whole face and shone through her hazel eyes, so that Duggie suddenly knew everything was going to be all right.

"I've brought the little suitcase with your odds and ends in it," Mrs. Tower said to Mrs. Brown, as the taxi drove off. Duggie went slowly back into the kitchen to look at the plaice.

Chapter Ten

A DAUGHTER was born to Mrs. Brown three-quarters of an hour after her arrival at the hospital that night, and a few days later Mrs. Towers took Duggie and Fred to see her.

The two boys spoke little in the long cream ward, with the glorious array of flowers on the big oak table in the middle, and all the new mothers looking very clean in their pastel bed-jackets, or cardigans.

There was a faint smell of antiseptic hanging over everything, and the bustling starched nurses with their shining neat hair half-hidden by their little caps made the boys feel shy. Some mothers had their babies beside them in a cot, but not Mrs. Brown. Everyone, however, seemed pleased to see Duggie and Fred and glad that there was a new addition to the Brown family. The boys had not expected so much attention. Their mother looked very well and happy, propped up in the wide bed on spotless pillows. Her cheeks were pinker and whiter than Duggie remembered them being before.

"Well, love, we've decided to call her Rosemary, so I hope you will be pleased," said Mrs. Brown, kissing her children with more fondness than usual. "Ever so heavy she was, an eight-and-a-half pounder. Sister says she's a fine baby, and her eyes are that blue. Freddie, your coat doesn't half look shabby. We will have to buy you a new one after this." She had never bothered much about their clothes before. Duggie thought this sudden interest must somehow be connected with Rosemary's arrival. In fact, Mrs. Brown was very conscious of the eyes of the other mothers on her children.

"Would you like to come now and see your little sister? She's just next door," said a nurse with fair hair and bright brown eyes.

They went through into a room full of cots. Looking at their occupants, it seemed to Duggie that all babies looked alike. But Rosemary, after all, was different, for her face was full of wrinkles and her eyes a wonderful periwinkle blue. Fred was worried about the wrinkles. "Makes her look old," he said. But the nurse relieved him of anxiety. "It's just that her bones and flesh haven't grown big enough for her skin yet. She'll be all right in a day or two, as chubby as all the rest put together, you'll see," she told the two boys. Duggie wondered if the babies often got mixed up, and then he noticed that each cot had a label with the parents' name on it. The Brown's had Stroughton Street, too, and he supposed that was because Brown is a common name.

"Your mother will have the baby with her all day from tomorrow onwards. It's only just at the beginning that we keep them in here," explained the nurse, smiling at the two children with her kind eyes. "Hasn't Rosemary a lovely skin? Come on, feel her hand, just touch it."

It was very warm and pink.

"Well, what do you think of her?" asked their mother when the two children were back in the ward.

"She's lovely," said Duggie.

"Aren't you proud to have a little sister?" said one of the other mothers.

"It'll be nice for Jennie," Duggie told them.

"And for me, too," said Freddie, leaning against Mrs. Brown's bed. He didn't seem quite so embarrassed by the whole affair as Duggie was, not so conscious of all the eyes in the ward, although most patients had their own visitors, seemed to rest on the boys all at once at the same moment. No one else seemed to have children to see them.

"Well now, go back to Bertha, and ask her to come in for a few minutes will you? I'm not really allowed more than one person at a time," said Mrs. Brown, and the boys went back to the waiting-room and sat in silence while Mrs. Towers went to see their mother.

"Wonder where she'll go," said Duggie at last.

"With Mum and Dad at first, I expect," replied Freddie.

"Wonder what they'll say at school when we tell them?"

"Noffink," said Freddie.

Wonder what Jane will think. I must tell Old Jock. He'll be pleased it's a girl, thought Duggie.

When they got home Mrs. Towers stayed to get the children's tea, and put Mr. Brown's supper ready, and then she went back to her house. Duggie went to see Old Jock and tell him the news. Tammy had been given a day of rest, and his master had spent most of the day in bed. Duggie made Old Jock a cup of tea and then he cleaned the harness. He thought a great deal about Rosemary. If only they could get a new and larger flat, life, he felt, would be perfect, but what was Dad doing about it? He longed for more freedom of movement at home, and more chance of getting away to read by himself sometimes. When Duggie had finished cleaning the harness, he gave the donkey a last feed and drink, and then he went to see Pete.

" 'Ullo, stranger! Watcha Dug," Pete said. "Where've you been all this time? Still with the old donk?"

"That's right. I'm entering for a race on him. And I've got another sister. That's what I came to tell you

—Rosemary, born last week, a smashing baby," said Duggie.

"Doesn't seem fair. You've got Jennie already. I've got no one, but just myself. I'm going to speak to my parents," said Pete seriously.

"Bad luck for you," agreed Duggie. "Other thing I wanted to know, was whether you know anything about the Smithson gang."

"Three of them you mean, brothers?"

"That's right."

"They come from the Paddington Canal. Rough lot they are. Their father's in prison and so's the elder brother. Mum knows because her friend Mrs. Eulkes lives there, see—on the Canal, I mean—mental she says they are, destructive for no reason."

"They tried to beat me up, after they had been stoning Tammy," Duggie told his story.

"I should keep clear of them, mate," advised Pete. "The elder brother half-killed someone. They don't go to school half the time if they can help it."

Duggie felt uneasy at this news. Peter never exaggerated, and Duggie didn't want to be half-killed.

"What did they want to come over here for?" he asked at last.

"I dunno. Maybe there's more to destroy round here, a bit more respectable than the canal, and the people aren't so quick with bicycle chains and knives in these parts."

"I'll just have to be looking out," said Duggie. "You're going round with Dick Rivers now, aren't you?"

"Yes, we're friends, seeing you were so busy with the donkey. His mother's a dressmaker, did you know? She's a widow. They have a smashing flat, three lamps in their sitting-room, and television, and

Dick's got his own radio, and he has five shillings a week pocket money."

"I don't get any," said Duggie ruefully.

"And if you did it would only go on the donkey," laughed Pete.

"I'll be getting back now," said Duggie, feeling suddenly oceans apart from his friend, who he realised was being subtly influenced by the more refined way of life practised by the Riverses.

"Hi, are you going in for the Eleven Plus Exam? Dick and I are. What does your Mum say?" Pete asked.

"Doesn't care either way. I shall ask Jane."

"Jane? Who's Jane?"

"A friend."

"What, have you got a girl friend? Not Jane Roberts? No need to be cagey."

The last word must have come from the Riverses' household, Duggie thought, looking at Pete's narrow, handsome face.

"She's grown up and she's helping me. Now I must be off. So long."

"So long, mate," said Pete, turning back into the dim hallway.

The next day Old Jock pulled ten pound notes out from the stuffing of his mattress and gave them to Duggie.

"Now go along and get a money order from the post office and enter the donkey for the big race before it will be getting too late. I'm looking forward to our wee gamble," said Old Jock. In spite of his slow way of speaking, he was obviously excited.

"O.K.," said Duggie, and he stuffed the notes into the left-hand pocket of his grey shorts, and set out at once whistling, "Whatever Will Be, Will Be," as he went. Just at that moment life seemed perfect; he had

74

a sister called Rosemary and he was going to ride in a Donkey Derby and Old Jock was better, and his mum would soon be back. Meanwhile, Mrs. Towers was cheerful, and cooked the best bacon and eggs he had ever eaten.

As he crossed the railway line, he heard the scuffling of feet in a side street behind him, but he paid no attention. Life seemed too good for worries just now. He had never bought a postal order before and, because ten pounds seemed a lot of money, he didn't go to the little local post office which occupied a corner in a grocer's shop, but headed for a larger one on a busy road, about half a mile from Jock's basement.

Presently he turned down an alleyway, with the railway on one side, and a few tiny deserted back gardens on the other. No one seemed about, but he didn't notice that either. He didn't notice anything in particular, until suddenly he heard a low cry. "So you squealed to the police did yer? You narked," and the next moment Frankie and the middle boy who wasn't George were upon him.

"We'll teach yer to nark," they said.

"I didn't tell anyone. Honestly, I didn't," gasped Duggie, and then his hands met the hard tarmac in the alleyway.

"So yer narked about your ruddy donkey. Yer narked ter the bogeys," Frankie's voice sneered again. "We'll teach yer to nark."

"Give 'im a chance," said the other boy. "Yer ain't sure." He stood up, and there was only Frankie to fight. In that second Frankie hesitated, and Duggie wriggled and wrenched and got on top of Frankie. He felt a wild surge of triumph as he pinioned the boy's arms. But the next moment that was lost for the other boy came in again then. "Don't yer 'urt Frankie," he said. Now the three of them rolled in a bunch on the

75

ground, a struggling panting mass of human flesh. They got nearer and nearer to the wire fence and then suddenly they were against it, and the lower strand was giving way against their weight. Duggie could feel it bulging out towards the railway line, and he couldn't hold back for the bodies of the others were forcing him outwards with the wire.

"The line," he gasped. "The railway line." He felt one boy hold back and then the next minute Frankie and he were rolling over and over.

Rosemary, he thought, and the Derby, and now it'll all be finished, finished. He tried to stop falling but he couldn't. He felt a sudden sense of futility. What did it all matter? He grabbed at stray strands of grass but mostly the ground was blackened earth. The thick black lines came nearer; a train whistled. He saw the white steam and smoke from an engine approaching at speed, a second before he hit the bottom, and then he felt a bump as Frankie landed on top of him, and the next moment he rolled into a ball and shut his eyes as a train raced by on the other line. Its hiss and its clatter of turning wheels faded into the distance, and he realised he was still alive. He unrolled, saw the signals were down and leapt to his feet.

"Better run for it," he said. "Are you all right?" For a few seconds the quarrel was forgotten, and then Duggie looked up and saw the third boy on his knees on the slope down which the two had rolled a few seconds before. The third boy was filling his pocket with bits of paper.

"What are you doing?" called Duggie, and then all at once the truth dawned on him. "Hi, my pound notes. Hi, thief. You can't do that. They're Jock's. They're not even mine. They fell out as I rolled down, must have . . ." he was becoming incoherent as he clambered up the steep, slippy slope.

"Rich, aren't yer? That'll teach yer to nark. We're made, Frankie, made!"

The next second a window opened.

"Come off the embankment. Children are not allowed there. Haven't you seen the notice? I'll call a policeman," a female voice shrieked.

The next minute Frankie and he were rolling over and over

"Scram, Frankie," said the third boy briefly and, picking up the last pound note, he scrambled to the top and ran off down the alleyway.

Duggie turned to try and trip Frankie but somehow that boy had got ahead of him too, and in a moment he had reached the top and set off in pursuit of his brother. And suddenly Duggie was alone and utterly routed.

"I don't know what to do," he said aloud. "I don't know what to do. I can't go back to Jock."

He felt this was the worst thing which had ever happened. He saw the pound notes coming out of the dark stuffing in the faded striped mattress, the gnarled hands giving them to him, counting them out. He relived the whole scene in the basement room.

"He's so poor," he said, "so poor."

He couldn't go back so he started to walk, purposelessly, without caring where he went. He considered consulting Jane, longed to tell someone of his fight, but he was afraid she would think he wanted her to advance the ten pounds and she would be embarrassed. It had been bad enough with the elderly woman in the Crescent.

At last he decided there was only one thing to do, to go to the Paddington Canal and find the Smithson Gang and persuade them to give him back the ten pounds. Surely if they realised the importance of the race they would think better of their theft, he reasoned, and, anyway their parents might be more honest. But dare he go alone? On second thoughts he decided not: he would go in search of Pete and tell him the whole story. Pete had never let him down in an emergency yet, and Pete was a strong fighter, though slow to anger and slight of build.

Chapter Eleven

RAIN STARTED to fall in a light silver drizzle as the two boys made their way towards the Canal.

"Supposing there's the three of them there?" asked Pete, who had not been easily persuaded to come.

"P'raps George is in prison," suggested Duggie. "Wonder how they came to think I had been to the police and informed."

They crossed a main road teeming with traffic, with great red trolley buses and rows of shops, and came into a dirtier area. Everywhere now they saw peeling stucco, broken windows patched clumsily with rag or cardboard, cracked paintless window frames, dreary terraces of filthy houses. Here and there a television mast rose sharply towards the grey heavens from some neglected roof top, unsure and incongruous in this decaying world of crumbling bricks and mortar. In the background they heard the scream of a circular saw and they smelt the cleanness of newly-planed wood. A Jamaican, dark as chocolate, wheeled a green barrow and smiled as the boys passed—a gash of pink and white in a face of ebony. Beyond him they saw 'Down With the I.R.A.' chalked unsteadily on a grey wall which had once been part of a house, and above their heads 'The Londoner's Opportunity,' a plum-red notice advertising evening classes.

They came to a bridge, where a blackboard said Rags 28/- cwt.—Wool 1/- lb., and a short man of swarthy countenance cut clothes into strips with a long knife in the murky depths of a dark shed.

They crossed the bridge, looking down at the

moored barges and the long lovely stretch of water, and the trees green now with spring. And they saw opposite them a battered row of tall houses with wrought-iron balconies, with broken doors and railings, with peeling walls, naked of paint, shouting of decay and dereliction. Outside these houses, on the wet mud, stood stinking dustbins, old boxes and discarded prams. Here and there broken masonry, gaping windows and shattered roofs reminded the world of Hitler and his bombs. And beyond all this, farther down the dark waters, stood whiter houses with gleaming palisades and grassy gardens, and graceful painted pillars just visible to the boys' wandering gaze.

"The Smithson gang live somewhere in that row," said Pete at last, pointing to the dreadful scene before them.

"Let's go," said Duggie, conscious of a quaking stomach and knees like water. God help us, he thought.

At that moment a young woman in a grease-spotted wool frock the colour of laurel leaves, with a red kerchief over her head, came out through a front door which had once been part glass and was now heavily patched with tin. She bent down to empty a pail of garbage into one of the bins, and Duggie called and asked which house the Smithsons lived in.

"Number 8, ground floor, darling," she answered with a friendly smile, which made Duggie feel suddenly more at ease.

Most of the numbers had long ago disappeared from the doors, however, and it was some minutes before they located number 8, the door of which stood ajar, showing a bare passageway, with damp brown walls, half-blocked by an ancient bicycle and a broken rush-seated chair. There was no bell or knocker and the two boys rapped with their knuckles on the rotten wood, and called, "Hallo, there." But there was no reply, nothing but silence in that house.

"Let's go. They're not here," said Pete without trying to keep the great relief he felt from his voice.

"Oh no, let's stay a little longer. They may turn up any minute," argued Duggie, thinking desperately of Old Jock's ten pounds. How could he begin to tell him?

"If only there had been a witness you could have gone to the police, but it'll be just your word against theirs," said Pete.

"I can't go to the police. Look at Tim, how he suffered through it and all, and landed up in that juvenile court, I don't want anything taking up my time before that Donkey Race."

"Well, you won't be able to enter at this rate," said Pete kicking a stone across the road with sudden angry impatience. "Come on, let's get back."

They turned and saw with a shock their two enemies walking coolly down the road towards them. At this moment it seemed impossible to Duggie that he would retrieve the ten pounds. These boys looked too nonchalant, too self-assured and pleased with themselves to suffer defeat. They were on home ground and their neighbours were at hand should they need assistance in battle.

"We should have ambushed them, taken them by surprise," whispered Duggie, feeling for the first time his inexperience in this kind of warfare.

"You had better do the talking. I'll back you up if it comes to a fight," Pete said. "Too late to make plans."

The Smithsons had almost reached them now. Frankie's eyes narrowed in a leer as he saw Duggie, and his brother, Jim, let out a low whistle which was somehow half insult.

"Can I have that money back?" Duggie said. "It didn't belong to me. But to an old man, who's poor and ill and sent me to buy a postal order with it. I can't replace it."

"Tell us annuver!" jeered Jim. "Next time you steals look after it, see. You can't 'ave it back anyway, cos it's spent."

Duggie felt a hot glow creep up his neck and spread across his face; it was a deep blush of anger. "I swear I didn't steal it. I had it from the rag-and-bone man, Old Jock. He's expecting the postal order. Come on, give us it back."

"What do yer mean, give it back? Jim's jest been telling yer it's spent, gorn," said Frankie.

"Let's look in your pockets then," suggested Duggie stepping with outstretched hand towards Jim. "Come on, turn them out."

The next second he went reeling backwards from a smashing blow on the chin which sent his head spinning. So this is it, he thought. We'll have to fight, and then he saw Pete lunge forward with a right hander, and he straightened himself and turned to settle Frankie. And now the fight was on in earnest, blow for blow—only the Smithsons weren't straight: they kicked below the belt if they could. But this time it was two against two; there was hope of winning and all Duggie's anger and frustration was behind his punches; he felt a wild exultation when he got his arm round Frankie's neck and started to force him back and back towards the muddy patch of ground. Gone now was the leer from the enemy's face, a sudden fear replaced it. The eyes were those of a rabbit caught in a trap, the trembling that of coward.

"You give me back that ten pounds or I'll, I'll . . ." threatened Duggie and then Frankie went down and for a second the triumph seemed almost complete.

Duggie's hands were on Frankie's shoulders, his knees on his stomach, and the Donkey Derby once again in his reach. And then across the stretch of London mud came Pete's sudden warning, "Look out, duck, duck," and as he flattened a milk bottle whizzed over his head, missing his scalp by a fraction of an inch. He looked up and saw, in quick despair, Jim with an armful of milk bottles and Pete with blood on his face. In his own triumph Duggie had forgotten his friend fighting the bigger foe. And now as he stopped to stare Frankie twisted beneath him. He turned back to subdue him and then he heard Pete yell once more, and the next moment something heavy hit his head, the world became bright with stars of gold and crimson and then there was darkness.

When he came round, Pete was kneeling at his side and the Smithsons had gone. It was still daylight. His head was going round in dizzy circles.

"You've only been out a couple of minutes," said Pete. "The others have gone."

The tall houses stopped leaning towards him; the ground became level. He started to remember the dismal happenings of the day, and shut his eyes again, not wishing to think about the loss of Old Jock's ten pounds.

"I don't know what I'm going to do," he said at last. And then he looked at his friend and saw the three scratches running down his cheek, and a spattering of blood.

"What's happened to you? How did he do it?" he asked.

"When I went in at him I didn't realise he had drawing pins between the fingers of his left hand, the one he didn't hit you with. He drew it down my face and these are the scratches. I fell back for a minute and he saw you bring Frankie down and then, before I could stop him, he had made for the milk bottles," Pete explained. "I couldn't get near him after that."

"We're not made for this sort of thing. We don't know how to do it. We should have come armed. Pete, I'm sorry," said Duggie clambering to his feet. "I shall have to go back and tell Jock. And what will your mother say when she sees your face? I've got an egg on my head, but Mum isn't there."

They made their way quietly homewards, past a turf accountant's, past low houses with damp basements, past two marmalade cats. They walked on in the silence of the defeated.

Somewhere they took a wrong turning and they came out into the busy road where Duggie had searched in vain for a taxi not many days before.

They looked a battered couple and they dragged their feet, ashamed at being so easily beaten. Duggie's sleeve had been torn by Frankie; his back and the seat of his shorts were covered in mud. People began to look at the two boys in disgust, for this was a more respectable road where fights were rare even between children. Duggie was dreading his return to the basement room. How would he break the news to Old Jock? His mind framed words and they all seemed utterly unconvincing. He wondered whether the old man would think he had made off with the ten pounds. The Smithsons' cool assumption that the money was stolen had unnerved the boy. The idea was unbearable. Yet the truth was almost unbelievable. A daylight robbery by children who had no reason to know he was carrying the ten pounds? It seemed a tall story, the unwarranted attack even more unlikely. "I am sorry, Jock, but something terrible has happened. I haven't entered Tammy, because . . ." Duggie began in his mind for the third time, and came to a halt. Oh

God, he thought, please do something. Don't let this happen.

The rain fell harder, gurgling in the gutters, dripping from the rooftops, and the sky took on the darker grey of dusk.

He looked very debonair

"Someone is grinning at you," said Pete in his quick decisive voice. "Never seen him in my life before."

Duggie looked up from the wet pavement and saw a pair of eyes he knew, the black rim of a bowler, a mouth which smiled. It was the young man who helped him get a taxi, and he said, "Hallo! What on earth have you been up to? Is your mother all right? You got there in time? No babies on the doorstep?"

He looked very debonair. He had a young woman

hanging on his arm, a girl in her twenties. She was tall and graceful with swinging dark hair, and they could smell her scent.

Duggie didn't know which question to answer first. "We bin fighting," he said at last.

"This is Miss Angela Freeman," said the pale face below the bowler hat. "What do you want to fight for?"

"Ten pounds—they stole it from me, and it isn't mine."

"Why? Oh, your poor face," exclaimed Angela seeing Pete for the first time.

"Leave this to me," said the young man. "Come on, tell us the whole story, perhaps we can help again. Funny how I keep running into you."

He was a very gullible person, Pete thought, for he seemed to hang on Duggie's words and believe everything. He had in fact been done several times in life, and cared little for money. They could not have met a better friend at that moment.

"And now I've got to tell Old Jock, and he'll be so upset, and I'm afraid he won't believe me. He'll think I've invented the whole story and spent the money on myself," Duggie finished.

"Can't we help, Mark? Can't we lend the money or something?" Angela seemed gushing to the two boys, but nice and definitely on their side, and they eyed her hopefully.

"I don't see why we shouldn't become the joint sponsors. I think it would be rather fun to enter a donkey. Have you got a form with you?"

Duggie delved in his pocket and handed Mark a very crumpled entry form in an envelope. "Yes, I took it to the post office with me, or rather I meant to. Here it is," he said. I shall always believe in miracles now, he told himself, in Good Samaritans.

"It would be a thrill to have a stake in a donkey. I'm free at Whitsun. We could go and watch. Oh, you poor people with your poor face and head. Can't we send the police to deal with the boys by the Canal?"

"One thing at a time, Angela, for heaven's sake! Let's look at this form first," said Mark. "What's the donkey's name?"

"Tammy."

"And yours?"

"Douglas Brown."

"I think it would be fun to back someone in this race. We'll go to watch it together." He was filling in the form as he spoke.

"Thank you, sir," said Duggie, so pleased that the money would get to the organisers in time that he thought of nothing else.

"Half a mo. I'll write a cheque now, and then we'll only have to get a stamp from that slot machine and it will be all done," said Mark, striding off towards a convenient post office, the one in fact to which Duggie should have gone to get his postal order.

"I want a stake in it, too. It was my idea," said Angela, hurrying after him.

"All right, you can pay me back something. I say, I hope the donkey *is* really fast. We should really have a look at him before risking a tenner. He's not on his last legs or anything, is he?" asked Mark.

"I'll take you to Tammy now if you like. He's jolly fast. He kept up with the horses in the Row."

"I've said we'll be at Mummy's by half-past six and it's ten to seven now, sweetie," Angela put in. "I don't think we've time to see anything now."

"All right. Give us the details of the race, will you? Ah, I see we get a free car park, as we are sponsoring an entry. I say, aren't we smart? How long is it to Whit Monday?"

"Seventeen days," said Duggie, who had been counting them frequently.

The letter disappeared through the slot in the red pillar box.

"Now you are really entered, just in time. The secretary will get it to-morrow. The deed is done," laughed Mark. "Come on, Angela, it would be splendid if we won a hundred guineas."

"Darling, you are being reckless. I mean, we haven't even seen the donkey. But I do love a gamble. Will you give us the address in case we have time to pop down and see Tammy?" asked Angela. "One minute we are walking along the road quite calmly and the next we are sponsoring a donkey. I must say life with you, darling, seems fun. Something extraordinary always happens when we are out together."

"Now put down that address. Then we must hurry, because your mother will be fuming," said Mark, handing her his pen.

"No ink."

"Lick on it then."

"S-T-R-O-U-G-H-T-O-N," spelt Angela. "Now the donkey's address."

Presently they were drifting away together beneath the black umbrella down the wide wet road.

"Well, of all the luck? Are you happier now?" began Pete.

"Aren't they nice? But didn't they talk? My head is aching like anything. Feel the bump."

"It's bigger," agreed Pete, running his hand through Duggie's thick fair hair.

They started back and, as they walked, Duggie realised the problem was by no means solved. They had entered the donkey in time, but they hadn't brought back Old Jock's money. He wouldn't win anything if Tammy won: the young couple would have it all. Duggie had used them as an expedient to gain time. The responsibility for the money weighed heavily on him. He considered the police again, but it was against his nature and upbringing to summon their help, and he was afraid of their questioning. How slender and unconvincing his story would sound, and how much more believable would be the defence put forward by the experienced Smithsons.

"I'll tell him the money's been sent. I've entered the donkey," he said aloud at last. "I hope he won't ask any more questions."

"You've seventeen days to think of something," Pete reminded him. "The old man will believe you. Of course he will."

Now the boys had come to their parting of ways.

"Thanks for everything. I'm sorry about your face, about the whole day," Duggie said.

"That's all right. Sorry you got in a mess. Be seeing you." Pete started up the hill, and Duggie turned down the narrow street which would take him to the high houses, and Old Jock's basement.

Chapter Twelve

DUGGIE DIDN'T tell Old Jock the whole truth. He couldn't bring himself to do so. He said ten pounds had been posted and the entry made, and that was all, and then he concentrated his efforts on training himself and the donkey for the race. For he felt the gods were with him and told himself another miracle must happen to solve the problem of the lost ten pounds. The sudden meeting with Mark and Angela in the street and their readiness to co-operate were more than a coincidence, he thought.

Now he was back at school and he rode mostly in the evenings, and he enlisted the help of Jane. Every other day she came to the bombed site and instructed him in the grey twilight, teaching him to sit properly, to increase and decrease the donkey's speed with the lightest aids and to circle and turn on the forehand, and to rein-back. Tammy was getting the schooling of a horse and he benefited from it. He became more supple and obedient and more confident in his rider. Jane was determined that the boy and donkey should be quick off the mark. Again and again she would stand with raised hand, saying "Ready, steady, go!" and dropping her hand on the last word, so that Duggie learned both to watch and listen, for they had no idea how the entries would be started and Jane thought they should be prepared for all possibilities.

On the days they didn't school the donkey Duggie would take him for a ride, as Jane said he needed change and must not get stale before the race. He didn't see the Smithsons and he supposed they considered the acquisition of ten pounds a just revenge for what they imagined he had done to them. After Whitsun he proposed to get his own back, though so far, he had no idea how this was going to be done.

There was, however, one difficulty which arose constantly and that was the existence of a bay pony with whom Tammy seemed to have fallen in love. She stood at a street corner with her gaily-painted trolley laden with vegetables and fruit from eleven to half-past six every day, and the donkey would bray with joy when he saw her and refuse to go by. She was a lovely animal with dark eyes in a delicate head, a glistening white star and a sleek coat which shone like mahogany, and the boy could not help sympathising with Tammy. After all, he reasoned, it must be a dull life for a donkey living alone day and night without kith or kin and it was not surprising he wanted a friend so badly. But Jane thought otherwise. Tammy, she said, must be obedient in all ways. If Duggie gave in to him in one way he would expect it over another and would jib in the race and be last.

It was the only point on which the boy and the librarian disagreed. Jane thought Duggie should agree with her because he was only an inexperienced child and couldn't know as much about riding and life as she did. But the boy could not bear to hurry the donkey past the beloved pony without letting them blow down their noses at each other. He was pleased that Tammy should have a friend at last, and he ignored Jane's instructions that he should use a stick on the donkey. He just pretended to be a feeble and hopeless rider whenever they had to pass the bay mare at the corner and let the two converse as long as they liked.

Apart from this, all preparations for the race were going smoothly. Old Jock had bought a hundredweight of oats and two bales of the best hard mixture hay, and Tammy was being fed better than ever before in his life and consequently becoming a much more lively mount. Flora and Toby were back in the stall, and the librarian and the rag-and-bone man seemed on good terms with one another. Joan Worthington-Smith had written a letter to Duggie wishing him luck, and Pete at last showed interest in the donkey and the coming race, and even brought Dick Rivers to watch the schooling on the bombed site one evening.

"Of course he won't win," said Duggie, over and over again. "But it will be fun to ride in a race."

Mark and Angela seemed to have disappeared from their lives as suddenly as they had come into them, and the boys began to wonder whether they would really come to the race and support their entry. The second meeting in the road, the signing of the cheque and the posting of the letter all seemed like a dream to Duggie now. It had happened so suddenly and unexpectedly.

His mother came back with Rosemary after another five days in hospital, and the Browns' rooms were terribly overcrowded. The Health Visitor, a pale young woman with a bun, was determined they should have a Council Flat, one of the new ones in the South Paddington district, and because she spoke in authoritative tones Duggie imagined she would arrange matters in the next month or so. He took Tammy down to see Rosemary, and Jennie and Fred had a ride on the donkey's back. Mrs. Brown patted him but was very absorbed in the new baby and Duggie didn't tell her about the race, partly because of this and partly because he was afraid she wouldn't let him go. The actual day was all right, he was sure, but there was the time it would take him to ride the fifty-five miles over there, for which he was going to allow the Friday, Saturday and Sunday. Not even Jane knew about that. Only Jock had been told and he believed in the spirit of adventure, and didn't think it was wrong for a boy of ten and a donkey to roam the roads for three days on their way to a race.

In addition to all these preparations, Duggie had the Eleven Plus examination to think of. Mr. Brown had suddenly announced that he expected Duggie to pass and go on to a grammar school. Mr. Brown would never have passed anything himself and had not shone at school, but that only made him the more anxious that Duggie should win through and have a good education.

"What does it matter when I only want to work on a farm?" the boy had asked. But Jane pointed out it

92

meant he would be able to go on to a university and study agriculture properly or to a special college which would give him a diploma. And then he would get a proper salary, instead of just a weekly wage, and be able to keep a horse to ride himself. She kept recommending books in the library which she thought might help him pass the examination, for which he would have to sit in July, twenty-five days after his eleventh birthday. With Jane and his father both suddenly interested, Duggie began to feel nervous. Before he had never worried about the exam. Now he thought about it constantly and at night he went over the day's lessons again before he slept.

All the time the day of the race was getting nearer and nearer, and the donkey was getting harder and fitter and Old Jock spent longer and longer polishing the bridle and grooming Tammy's coat while Duggie was doing his best at school.

Then one evening a week before Whitsun Jane brought Duggie a pair of cord jodhpurs.

"They belonged to one of my cousins. They've been lying in the hall chest there for years, and they smell of both balls, I'm afraid," she said. "Go into the stall and pop them on and let's see how you look in them."

They fitted round the waist but were too long in the legs.

"Will your mother take them up for you?" she asked. "You look a bit like a clown."

Duggie thought for a bit and decided she probably wouldn't. If she had known about the race and approved she might have done so, but, as it was, she would put them aside until she had a spare moment and months might pass before a single stitch was sewn. He considered saying "Yes," and then asking Mrs. Towers to make the alteration, because he didn't want to let his mother down, but at last he decided that might not be effective either.

"She's so busy with Rosemary, you see. That's the trouble," he said at last.

"Never mind. I'll do it. Didn't I see an old piece of chalk lying about here the other day? Yes, here we are. We'll mark them like the proper tailors do."

Jane took them home with her that night, and next day Duggie rode in them for the first time. He wished he could repay her for all she had done for him in some way, but he couldn't see how. He had been helped so much by people in the last few months, and on thinking it over he decided that perhaps the loss of the ten pounds and the devilish Smithsons were to counteract that in some way. You couldn't have good luck all the time. It was always balanced somehow with bad, he decided. If the Browns got the Council Flat at once it would probably mean he wouldn't win the race. After all, they had got Rosemary, and that must be all the good luck they could expect as a family for at least a month or two. Except, of course, the race and nothing would really make him rule that out completely, because it had become too important a dream to him.

And so the last Thursday came and they gave Tammy one short gallop in the bombed site and that was all. Pete and Dick and Old Jock and Jane came to watch. They cheered and clapped to get the donkey used to the noise of spectators.

Jane was going away for Whitsun with her mother, but hoped to get to the race somehow. Duggie couldn't look her straight in the face any more, because he had lied to her, and muttered about horse-boxes and trains when she asked how he was taking Tammy to Selbury Towers, instead of telling the truth. She had not questioned him further and he supposed she imagined Old Jock was paying, but really she had noticed his embarrassment and decided to drop the subject. He was afraid if he told the truth she would think him too young to go so far alone and try to persuade him to forego the ride over.

And then it was Thursday night and he was in bed and unable to sleep, because the race was so near. And then suddenly it was dawn and he could hear the clanking of milk bottles at the end of the street, and he rose slowly to dress.

Chapter Thirteen

AT LAST he was on his way, riding through a May morning, truant from school for one day, with all the endless traffic pouring into London passing him in one ceaseless roar.

Tammy moved with the lowly unhurried shuffle of his kind, a two-mile-an-hour walk, Duggie supposed—and what did time matter? The boy was happy riding through the bright gold of the sun, with all the long day before him, and the next, and the one after that, before Monday and the race. Each step took him away from the noisy haste of London to the quieter greener places. He began, as noon came, to see woods deep and cool, beyond the long row of houses, and low hills of grass, and in the suburban gardens the pink apple blossom floated confetti-like to grace the turf of lawns or to lie between the green stalks of the daffodils.

With Jock he had studied the map with minute care, finding the quieter roads which would be more pleasant for Tammy and himself, and, when he came to Spindly Church and the Basket Maker's Arms, he knew to turn down a winding side road where the thorn hedges were bright with dog roses and wild meadow-sweet decked the banks in white.

And now it was time to continue his journey and as he rode on down the sunlit road of May, he thought of his mother reading the note he had left her. He saw his uneven, carefully rounded handwriting on the lined paper torn from an exercise book at school the day before—the words: *Gone to the Donkey Derby and shall be away four days, don't worry, Mum. Old Jock and the librarian will be there to see me race. I've money to buy food. Love to the baby and all—Duggie.*

She wouldn't call the police; he knew that. One of his uncles and a cousin had done time in prison. She didn't think of policemen as people to help her. She might go to the vicar; she never was seen in church, but when in trouble she always thought of the vicar first. He was tall, white-haired and kind, and he listened with tireless patience to his parishioners' tales of woe; and he always *acted*, Mrs. Towers said. But surely the only way he could act to bring Duggie home was to enlist the help of the police, and Mrs. Brown wouldn't stand that. She would probably go to Old Jock first, Duggie reasoned, and Jock would persuade her he and Tammy were quite safe together. He would talk about the spirit of adventure and everything would be all right. Or else she would be too busy with Rosemary to do anything at all. After all, he was ten now.

Soon he was hungry and he stopped at a little village shop and bought bread and cheese with the money Old Jock had given him for the journey, and begged a bucket of water for Tammy, from the fat, red-cheeked woman behind the counter.

"Not often we see a donkey in these parts. Do you

He rode on down the sunlit road of May

D

live round here?" she asked, and he noticed her voice was slow and her words drawn out compared with the Cockney talk to which he was accustomed.

"No, I'm new to the district," Duggie said. "I've some way to go yet."

He hurried on as soon as Tammy had drunk his fill, for fear that the woman might ask whether he had run away from him. He looked too pale to be a country boy and his voice would give him away as a Londoner. He hadn't a watch but farther on he asked a farm labourer the time. It was half-past two.

"That's a fine little donkey," said the labourer, getting off his bicycle. "Are you taking him to the races?"

"That's right," said Duggie, and then thinking the man looked friendly rather than censorious, "Can you tell me of anyone a few miles farther on who would put up a donkey for the night?"

The labourer took off his cap. "Well, there's Jack Smiles. He's a good sort. But he ain't got much room like, that's the trouble—not even for a donkey. So much land is up for hay this time of year," he said.

"I don't want Tammy to be in good grass or he will blow himself out and get slow," said Duggie, remembering Old Jock's instructions.

"Oh, ah, that's right. I'll tell you what, you try young Charlie Peterson. He's got a tidy bit of land. You'll see his place five miles on, a white farmhouse with a green outside and a pond, you can't miss it. Just follow the road, go through Naughton-under-Beechwood and it's the next village after that. But what about yourself?"

"I shall be all right in a barn. I'll fit in anywhere," said Duggie, beginning to move on. "Thanks a lot."

"Oh, so you've got some pluck then. Well, good luck, son." The farm labourer mounted his bicycle. "I daresay Mrs. Peterson could spare a bed for you. They're a 'ospitable lot up there."

"Thank you," said Duggie again, and then he was riding alone up the road, with the sun tracing patterns of gold before him, through the tangled canopy of leaves above his head.

Wonder if I will be biking down a road like this one day in Wellington boots with a cap on my head and bits of straw on my collar, he thought.

He passed through Naughton-under-Beechwood at five past three, leading the donkey, and at five minutes to four he saw a rambling white farmhouse with yellow rosebuds running riot on the walls and a great cedar standing by the gate. On the murky waters of the pond three Aylesbury ducks sailed with their ducklings. On the emerald green two nanny goats grazed, tethered to strong stakes hammered into the ground. And five spaniel puppies, fat as knitted toys, played in the low-walled garden close to the farmyard.

For the last hour and a half he had banked on the hospitality of the Petersons, but now he was here he felt shy. Should he knock on the front door or go through the five-barred gate into the farmyard? He saw five dairy cows waiting outside a byre, their bags heavy with milk. He supposed there were not enough stalls to go round; they had to wait their turn. He could hear the steady cackle of hens in a barn and somewhere a cock crowed. And he decided then on the farmyard. There seemed so much activity there.

He left Tammy tied to the gate and went to the long cowshed, where the electric milking machine was at work and the cows stood in a long row chewing the cud with quiet calm. It was some time before he was noticed and then a youngish man in a white coat came forward.

"What can I do for you?" he asked as though Duggie were grown up.

"I'm wondering whether you could put a donkey up for the night somewhere, please. He's only a little one," the boy said.

"Where is it?" His eyebrows went up as he spoke. "Did you say a *donkey*?"

"Outside, tied to your gate. He's entered for the big race."

"Never heard of a race for donkeys. Not round here is it?"

"No, it's about thirty-five miles farther on, at Selbury Towers."

"Oh, there. Are you all on your own then?"

"Yes, that's right. It's not till Whit Monday so I'm taking Tammy slowly. He's just outside. "

"Where do you come from, not from round here?"

"No, London," Duggie admitted reluctantly. "Tammy's a rag-and-bone donkey, really, but he's terribly fast too. I've been training him."

"Good for you. Yes, I suppose I can find a corner somewhere. I'll move the heifers out of the little paddock and he can go there. Bring him in, will you, while I finish off these cows. I've had a good many animals in my farm, but never one of those. You're not joking, are you?"

Duggie shook his head.

Presently the little grey donkey was grazing in a small square field, flanked by ragged elms, in which the birds sang. And beyond were green meadows climbing to meet a wooded slope and, higher still, the opal eastern skies of evening.

"And what about you?" asked Charlie Peterson.

"I thought I could sleep in the hay, if you don't mind," Duggie explained.

"There are only a few bales in the barn and they are

deuced hard, and the cattle won't like them much after you've put your muddy feet all over them."

"Would the straw be better?" The boy felt a little squashed.

"And who said I had some straw?"

"No one. I'll walk on and find a stack or something." Duggie realised now how little he knew about the country. In London people talked about sleeping in hay as though it was soft and loose, not baled and hard and prickly.

"Look, come indoors and have a word with the missus. She'll find you a glass of milk and something to eat, and we'll think about sleeping quarters later," said Charlie Peterson, with a sudden smile. "Quite sporting to ride so far to enter in a race. Are you a Cockney?"

He was beginning to laugh now, watching the boy's face.

Soon Duggie was seated at a large table in a cool stone-flagged kitchen telling the story of his life with Tammy and Old Jock, and their hopes for the big race on Whit Monday.

"And you've never had a proper riding lesson in your life?" Charlie said when he had finished.

"Well, Jane knows a good deal. She's taught me in the evenings."

"And where does your mother think you are now?" asked Mrs. Peterson, watching him with her big blue eyes.

"She knows I'm on my way because of the note I left, you see. She won't worry, because there's the new baby taking up her time. And she knows I can look after myself."

"I think we had better let her know you are here and safe," said Mrs. Peterson. "Otherwise she may tell the police to look for you and you'll never get to the race. She must be worried stiff."

"She's not on the telephone, and she won't worry—honest. Old Jock will put her mind at rest."

"He wouldn't put *my* mind at rest if you were my child," said Mrs. Peterson. "Isn't there a shop or something where we could leave a message?"

"I don't know whether Jones's are on the telephone. They are the grocers. Her best friend is Mrs. Towers, but she's got no phone. There's the vicar, she might have gone to him."

"Vicars are such busy people."

"Well, there's Dick; his mother's a dressmaker, so I suppose she's got a telphone, and he could tell Pete and Pete would take a message to Mum."

"That sounds complicated, but I suppose it's all right. Charlie and I have friends and relations between here and Selbury Towers. We'll be able to see you're fixed up with proper sleeping quarters, and to put your mother's mind at rest," explained Mrs. Peterson.

He was a little afraid they were going to take some of the fun out of his expedition. However, he looked up the telephone number of Dick's mother in the London directory, and Mrs. Peterson contacted her and arranged that Pete should go round to Mrs. Brown's and explain that Duggie was safe and well and would be found suitable stopping places for the next two nights of his journey to the races.

Duggie was given a boiled egg with his tea and there was real farm butter and home-made blackberry jam. Afterwards he went outside with Charlie Peterson and helped mix a feed of oats, bran and chaff for the donkey, who seemed happy and calm grazing alone in the paddock.

"How many years since he was last in a field, poor

beast, I wonder," mused Charlie, watching the white muzzle plunge into the bucket of food.

There was a black-and-white sheep dog called Lassie, as well as the spaniel bitch and her puppies, and Duggie spent the evening playing with all these dogs on the lawn beneath the cedar tree in the fragrant shady garden. He saw the sun setting in the western sky, a ball of fire beyond the wine-dark woods; he heard the gentle swish of the cows in the grass, and the strange cry of the guinea fowl, "Come back, come back," and above it all the bellowing of the red bull in his pen by the old barn. And he smelled the wet leaves and the earth when the dew came and saw the petals of the flowers closed in sleep.

And then it was time to go to bed and he was taken to his little room, where there was a wooden bed with a blue counterpane and a window looking out across the sleeping meadows. And he was told to have a bath first in the tiled bathroom and given a blue towel and a sponge and soap.

Night was blue at the window when he drifted into sleep; somewhere an owl hooted and over the quiet fields a fox came in search of food. And in his dreams he was lost and never reached the race-ground until it was all over.

Chapter Fourteen

THE LITTLE donkey gave a great bray of pleasure when Duggie came across the upland sweep of lawn to feed him next morning, as though the night had been too strange and too long in these unfamiliar pastures. He hurried forward, through the dew-wet grass beneath the tall elms bright now with sunrise, with pricked ears and hopeful happy eyes.

Duggie patted the hard short neck, pulled the long ears and ran his hand over the sharp spine with the black stripe running down it like a dark seam.

"We're lucky," he said. "Oh Tammy, we've been lucky! If only it will last! There's still Old Jock's ten pounds to worry about. If you win, he'll expect fifty guineas, plus the fiver I'm supposed to have borrowed from him. But surely there is some way round that problem."

He watched the donkey eating with slow patience, the white muzzle sifting the oats from the chaff with cunning skill, the small grey lips munching methodically. In the next field he could see four great pink sows with their curly-tailed piglets. The air was loud with their grunts, and when they coughed they were like humans.

When the donkey had finished, he tied him under a tree with his halter and then he went indoors to eat porridge, bacon and eggs, and toast, butter and marmalade. Mrs. Peterson said, "My husband has drawn you a map, so you can find your way to John Hillwood's place, and he's put a list of villages which you will have to pass through at the bottom. There are plenty of signposts, so you'll be all right. We rang John after you had gone to bed last night, and he'll put you up, so there's nothing to worry about. He's a nice man, is John, and Maisie's the homely sort."

"I've still got eighteen shillings and sixpence. Old Jock gave me some money, so I shall be able to pay, and please what do I owe you?" asked Duggie.

"Oh, forget it, dear; we've loved having you and we hope you have luck in the race. We don't want any money. I've made you a packet of sandwiches."

Duggie didn't know how to thank them, and he never liked good-byes. He was sorry to leave the spaniel, Laura, and her puppies and Lassie, the sheep dog.

But once on the road again, he thought only of Tammy and the race. And his eyes were only for the lovely fields around him gilded again with the golden sunlight, and the shining singing river which came suddenly in view like a silver ribbon winding through the browsing landscape. He heard the hum of bees and saw them black on the flowers in the bright gardens of summer, and, again and again, the triumphant cackle of a hen boasting of an egg just laid and the imperious crowing of some proud cock surrounded by his busy scratching wives.

At lunch time he took the donkey into a wide meadow and ate his egg sandwiches beneath a pale willow tree, which leaned with sad boughs towards its own reflection in the clear waters of a stream. Above his head a cuckoo called and below he saw a fish darting, blue and scaly.

This is the life for me, he thought, the land and the river, the sunlight and the clear skies of the country. And he watched the golden Guernseys grazing in the field next door, and, over the water, in a drier meadow, the white-faced sheep watching with hazel eyes their quick frolicking lambs playing with such abandon in the grass. London and his own grey street seemed a thousand miles away; at this moment they no longer existed for him. Only these meadows, these animals, these sights and sounds were important for him now, even the Race faded into nothing in this tranquil sunlit hour.

But he could not linger long. The donkey had eaten his fill, there were ten miles to be covered before dusk, and he hated hurry. He wanted his little mount to travel slowly and at ease, for he reasoned, the unfamiliar landscape, the sudden change from town to country, stall to meadow, must in itself be tiring for Tammy, who kept looking around with wonder and surprise.

In a little village, green with orchards, he stopped to give three tiny children a ride on the donkey's back, and to beg a bucket of water. Outside the post office a yellow poster advertised the Donkey Derby in large black lettering and all at once he was half-mad with excitement, and he had a sinking feeling in the pit of his stomach. Supposing he was last? Angela and Mark, Old Jock and Jane would all be disappointed. He wouldn't have to admit about the loss of the ten pounds, so long as the real sponsors didn't get together with the old man. He must keep them apart, but how? He would probably lose and then, after all, it wouldn't matter very much. Now he had seen the notice the whole affair seemed so much more important a function; he couldn't imagine himself the winning jockey.

People began to call out, "Going to the races? Good luck!" when they saw him walking by. He led Tammy mostly to rest his back. I'm only going for the fun of the thing, he thought.

Charlie Peterson's map was very clear and he had no difficulty in finding his way. At half-past three he came to the village of Hoppington and there by the grey stone church was John Hillwood's modern house and, all around, his pig-sties and his little fields divided and divided again by pig wire or electric fencing.

Duggie knew at once that he would never be Hillwood's type of farmer. He wanted the stretching acres the rolling meadows and shady paddocks of Peterson's place, not a muddled, overcrowded smallholding, and that modern dolls' house, looking so red and cheap beside the quiet dignity of the grey Saxon church.

He felt shy and nervous all over again as he led the donkey up the narrow gravel path to the brown front door and pressed the white bell. But his fears were short lived, for almost at once a brisk, brown-eyed woman in a flowered overall came round from the back of the house smiling and laughing. This must be Maisie.

"So you've got here? We do think you're sporting. God, I wish my kids had your guts. They won't go near a pony, only interested in machines, tractors, cars, aeroplanes, that sort of thing. Isn't it a dear little donkey? How old? Wait, and I'll go and see if there's a carrot." She disappeared into the kitchen again, and Duggie knew he would be all right here. There was no need to worry. She would do all the talking, and she was glad to have him. He knew that by the way she had looked at him. She liked children. It was something you could tell in a moment. He felt at home with her already.

She came back still laughing and Tammy munched the carrots and jingled his bit, and didn't tread on the flowerbeds.

"And you come from London? What part? How many miles have you covered so far? Have you ever ridden in a race before?"

Duggie soon realised she didn't expect half her questions to be answered. He replied to the last one whenever there was a pause in the conversation and that seemed to work very well.

Soon he was taken to a long low shed, in which a pen had been made for Tammy with hurdles in a corner. It was deeply bedded in straw, and there was an armful of hay and a bucket of water waiting for him.

"We only have pigs and hens, but we borrowed a little hay and a few oats for you. We are always helping out Captain Lake, so he doesn't mind doing the same for us occasionally. Will this be all right? He can go out later when the pigs are in if you like, but Charlie said you didn't want him to have too much grass. You're taking the race very seriously, aren't you? Have you been riding long?"

It was agreed eventually that it would be best for Tammy to spend the night inside, as he had already eaten a good deal of May grass, during the two rests Duggie had given him on the journey.

They left him peacefully eating and then they went indoors and Duggie helped Mrs. Hillwood prepare an enormous high tea with ham and salad, trifles, bread, butter and jam, and home-made cakes and biscuits.

Then he went back to the shed and groomed the donkey until John Hillwood, a thoughtful silent man, was ready to eat. The meal took a long time and Mrs. Hillwood managed to find out a great deal about Duggie's background in the course of it. She thought his house sounded very overcrowded, and his tea too scanty and his mother too happy-go-lucky.

"Doesn't she mind you just coming here on your own, doesn't she worry about you?" she asked for the third time.

"He's told you once, Maisie. Come out and have a look at the stock, son; they may interest you if you want to go into farming."

Duggie saw all the pigs, the Saddlebacks and the Sussex Whites and he saw the Rhode Island Red hens in the big barn on deep litter, and John Hillwood explained the artificial lighting system, which meant the hens were only in darkness for eight hours on a winter's night, instead of sixteen, and so laid a greater number of eggs. Duggie didn't approve of that system, though humans used it for themselves to live in. He thought Nature knew what she was about when she arranged night and day, and hens should not be denied their long sleep on winter nights. But he didn't say so; he remained silent after John Hillwood's explanation, which didn't seem to matter because the man so often remained silent himself.

In the fields next door there was the smell of the dying grass cut for silage, and he wished suddenly that nothing had to be cut or killed or trampled, that the little piglets would not be fattened into porkers for the table, and the deep litter hens not slaughtered at two years when they had passed their prime.

He had another bath that night before he went to bed in the small square room at the top of the narrow brown staircase. From his window he could see the church, looking squat and homely, and the green silage field, and beyond that a row of ugly modern houses with wire-fenced gardens devoid of trees. There was no owl hooting to-night, but he could hear the local inhabitants going to and fro from the white-washed pub and sometimes the baa-ing of sheep on some distant hill.

In the morning it was raining. People were going to Holy Communion under umbrellas or heavily clothed in mackintoshes. He wakened to hear the church bell ringing and the footsteps on the road, and the scream-ing of the pigs as John Hillwood fed them.

He knew he had overslept, for he had meant to help John early, but it didn't really matter because he only had ten miles to cover that day, and the Hillwoods were his friends and wouldn't mind. He made his bed carefully after he had washed and dressed and when he got downstairs Maisie was busy making toast and scrambling eggs.

"Run out and look at the donkey! He's brayed for you twice already," she said.

Tammy was looking very snug in the deep straw in

109

the little pen and, now that it was raining, Duggie was doubly pleased that they had not put him in the field. His coat was lying flat, though his thin mane needed a brush and there was manure on his strong narrow tail. The boy fed and watered him and went back to the kitchen.

After breakfast Mrs. Hillwood gave Duggie some black boot polish for cleaning the bridle.

"No point in starting yet when it's so wet. You haven't a mac, have you?" she said.

Later he groomed the donkey as best he could with an old piece of sacking—there were no brushes it seemed on this farm, and Mrs. Hillwood gave him some olive oil to make the hoofs look nice.

The sun came out suddenly, as the morning service began in church and the first hymn was sung, and a rainbow dipped across the sky, a delicate elusive band of many hues, as brightly coloured as a peacock's tail, and down in the fertile valley a horse neighed, a shrill blatant sound cutting across the hymn singing and the drowsing fields dotted with sleeping pigs.

At last it was time to go again. Mrs. Hillwood pressed an apple into Duggie's hands, and a little packet of home-made cakes, and she kissed him on the cheek and wished him luck. And her husband said, "I haven't telephoned Hugh Sampson, but he's a good sport. He's sure to put you up. His house is all black and white timber, you won't miss it, and he's got a pedigree herd of Jerseys, some of the best in the country. He's a rich man and it will be no trouble for his housekeeper to find room for you. Just mention my name, say you spent last night here, and he'll not refuse you."

It was a breezy, changing day, the skies transparent and the sunshine pale and fitful, and the little clouds tossing on the horizon like balls of cotton wool in a sea of chiffon.

The donkey was reluctant to leave his pen and he wouldn't hurry on the straight hot road, for he imagined he had another twenty miles to cover that day and he was bored.

Soon the kind undulating country gave way to flatter land crowded with houses and gardens. They came into suburbs and met tall green buses half empty. There were pavements now and street lamps, reminding the boy and donkey of London, and then suddenly the town itself basking in sunlight, and a climbing narrow street between old houses, busy with traffic. And here in the centre, crossing the road, Tammy decided he would go no farther. He put his head down, braced his forelegs and stopped with the suddenness of a braking car. And his habitual expression of calm and tolerance changed in a second to one of mule-like obstinacy. His eyes became more sunken and every inch of his body tautened in silent protest. He had gone far enough. Nothing would make him move.

Cars began to pile up behind. Horns hooted with raucous anger or blared or tooted; drivers leant out of their windows to advise, encourage or insult. Suddenly the street was in turmoil, the traffic was jammed and Duggie felt the sweat on his brow, as he tried all the ways of persuasion he knew. A kind woman brought young carrots from a greengrocer's shop, but Tammy was immune now to the temptation of food. Nothing would budge him. Duggie pushed and pulled, scolded and encouraged all in vain. Together the boy and donkey remained in the very centre of the street. A policeman came.

"We can't have you holding up the traffic. Come on, shift the little brute," he said gruffly, giving Tammy a smart slap on the rump.

111

"Come on there, get a move on. I've got a train to catch," another voice shouted impatiently.

"You've no right to bring an animal not under proper control into the town," the policeman said.

"He's never done it before," Duggie said, desper-

Nothing would budge him

ately dragging at the reins. He would never get to the Derby now.

"Get on and give him a beating," someone shouted.

The policeman moved off and started to control and direct the traffic, so at least one stream of cars could get through. Some of the passengers were laden with picnic baskets and children had buckets and spades with them, and Duggie realised then that this was one of the main roads to the seaside. The people must have waited until they were certain it wasn't going to be a wet day and then all started at roughly the same time. He vaulted on to the donkey and tried beating him with a broken piece of elm which he had used to hit at stray flies yesterday. It seemed his only hope.

A woman shouted, "Don't you do that, you cruel boy. I shall report you to the R.S.P.C.A. Fancy hitting a poor dumb beast."

"Leave him alone, ma'am. The animal must be mastered. We want to get to the seaside. Go on, boy, give 'im another," shouted a red-faced man in a trilby.

But Duggie didn't. He dismounted and tried again with the carrots, and then suddenly he heard the clatter of hoofs; a child came trotting up the road on a brown pony. The donkey pricked his ears; his legs relaxed; his eyes lit up. A sudden hush fell on the spectators in the cars.

"On your way to the races? Got stuck? Perhaps he'll follow Topsy," the girl on the pony called. She had red hair and a yellow shirt and pale green eyes. She brought her pony into a walk and went ahead of Tammy, and the donkey looked up and then began to walk too, and suddenly from the very depths of his being there came a hideous bray; it went on and on; it was louder and uglier than all the honking of all the horns; it ended at last in a noise which was half-hiccup and half-sob, and all at once all the drivers, all the spectators and all the passers-by burst out laughing.

Only Duggie and the girl remained serious.

"Keep following me. Jolly bad luck to be caught like that," said the girl.

But Tammy was happy now; he trotted along gaily behind the brown pony, which he somehow associated with his bay friend in London.

"Thanks," said Duggie. "You've saved me. I'll just jump on. He's going so fast now. It's hard to keep up."

The girl stayed with them for half an hour and they covered three miles in that time, and, when she turned off to meet a friend, Tammy didn't seem to mind after all. He hurried on as though he thought he would meet another pony soon and the world wasn't such a rotten place as he had imagined. But Duggie kept wondering whether he would do the same thing in the race, whether Jane had been right after all and Tammy should have been beaten past the bay pony with the gaily painted trolley. Supposing he jibbed right at the very start and wouldn't move at all?

He wondered and he worried until he told himself that neither would help him one scrap. After all he was only entered for fun. And then he saw the black and white house, looking clean and modernised in the mellow light of mid-afternoon, and he knew he had come to his third and last stopping place, and only the immediate present loomed large in his mind.

Chapter Fifteen

"No," the housekeeper said, "I've never heard of a Mr. and Mrs. Hillwood, and Mr. Sampson will *not* have stray animals amongst his pedigree cows, and that's straight, so I'm afraid you must go elsewhere begging your accommodation."

"But, Mr. Hillwood . . ." Duggie began again.

"I don't care who said you were to come here. It doesn't make any difference. This is one of the finest accredited herds in the district. You go and ask the cowman whether you can put a donkey in one of them fields and see *his* face!" She started to shut the door.

114

Duggie hated her fat shapeless figure bulging in grey; her sharp blue eyes behind the thick lenses and her ill-fitting false teeth. She was a bully who suspected the worst of everyone.

"I don't beg," he called, "I've got money to pay." And then he went back to the road and sat on the verge amongst the meadow-sweet and the yellow dandelions.

"Thank goodness I only asked for you, Tammy, and not myself too. I couldn't have spent a night in that house. It was far too smart. I could smell the richness of it."

After a bit he started to wander down a lane looking for barns or haystacks, and allowing Tammy to stop every few minutes for a graze on the bank. He was only a mile from the racecourse and he hoped to see donkeys, but he saw only the short-legged Jersey cows, with their big kind eyes and dear concave faces, and Sampson's expensive post and rails painted a shining white to match his house. Every gate was padlocked so he couldn't take Tammy into a field to offer him a drink at a trough.

"Can't expect luck all the way," he supposed, and turned back to the road once more where the thorn hedges were high and friendly and the land no longer Sampson's. And in a little wooded valley he saw a deserted barn and, beside it, a derelict house with broken windows and gaping roof. A narrow muddy track lined with ragged robin and bright climbing bramble leaves led there, deep into the dark wood and then out into the sunlight which lay on the clearing where the broken buildings stood. The grass around was green and lush; an old water butt was half-full of water and part of the barn was rainproof. It could have been a palace to Duggie at that moment. He explored the track farther and found it led to a field grazed by bullocks, and that, he supposed, accounted for there being some loose hay in a corner of the barn. It had been used for feeding the bullocks last winter and this was the remains. He sat down on the yellow-green pile and it was as he had imagined country hay would be, soft and sweet smelling, and then he knew everything was going to be all right. He would get to the Derby. Old Jock would be there ready with a brush to groom Tammy. The problem of the ten pounds would somehow be solved.

The boy grazed the donkey for three hours, and ate the bread and cheese he had bought on the way, and saw the sun setting vermilion and gold behind the valiant trees and far away the blue line of the sea. The last cuckoo called from the wild cherries and sparrows twittered in the gorse and dusk came fragrant with the scent of dew wet flowers. He tied the donkey to a post in the old crumbling barn and lay down in the hay, and tried to sleep. But thoughts of the morrow urged his brain to action and his eyes were still open when the pale moon climbed amongst her stars and cast down her silver upon the silent sleeping world, upon the donkey, lying with that Biblical look about him, a small tidy figure with four legs neatly tucked under the warm body and the long ears drooping as he drowsed. A shaft of silver light lay across his forehead, and illumined the black stripe across his back.

Turning and shivering a little on his bed of hay, Duggie knew London was no longer the place for him, now that he had seen and smelled and savoured this older, earthier world.

Morning came, bright and pearly, the pink sun rising above the eastern hills, the birds' dawn chorus flooding the woods with song. Down the track a labourer walked whistling the tunes of war-time and swiping the tall grass with a sprig of ash.

"Hallo, and who's here?" he asked, seeing the boy and donkey outside the buildings. "Not spent the night in them old buildings, have you?" He laughed when he spoke because it was Whitsun and he was free now till evening, and he was going to the races with his wife and children, and the day was fine.

Duggie told him the truth slowly, watching the weatherbeaten face for signs of friendliness or distrust.

"I hope I haven't spoiled the hay, and I want to buy some oats for Tammy or he won't have any life in him for the race," he finished. The man's face creased into a smile and the broad slow voice said, "Well, come you up to the cottage with me and the wife will find you a bite for breakfast, and maybe we can get something for the donkey too. You'll need a good brush before you ride in them races. You're covered in hay. I expect you're thirsty, ain't you?"

They went across the flat meadow together, the donkey, the boy and the man, and in a low thatched cottage Duggie had bacon and eggs and drank cups of milk with the labourer's three children, and Tammy was found some oats which the labourer had for his hens. Then Duggie cleaned the bridle on the green path by the young peas and lettuces. And Pauline, the eldest daughter, helped him and told him the name of her tortoise and the fox terrier which stood so importantly in the gateway, barking at passers-by.

Now the time of the Race was getting near and his hands shook when he thought about it and his brain would not concentrate. Pauline was impatient. "You're not listening. Do attend," she complained between the stories she told him, sitting on the sunlit path.

Presently he was riding to the race-ground, and Tammy seemed full of life, as though he knew something exciting was about to happen. And Duggie thought of all the people who knew about his entry in the race, whose thoughts might be with him: the Petersons and the Hillwoods, Mark and Angela, Jane and Jock, Pete and Dick, his mother and father, the

"Why didn't you say you were riding?"

old woman with the umbrella, and now this farm labourer and his family, who had promised to cheer him and to lend a hand if his London friends were delayed.

He turned off into a narrow road following an A.A. sign to "The Races" and suddenly cars and spectators were all around him and a little way ahead he could see white tents and the white rails of the course, and he could hear a voice on a loud-speaker blaring instructions. He felt a sinking in his stomach and a quickening of his pulses. And then he saw other entries stepping down from horseboxes and trucks, smart clipped donkeys prancing like ponies, and well-dressed children in jodhpurs and crash caps waiting to ride them. Now he knew he hadn't a hope. "It's only a bit of fun," he said aloud. "Oh, Tammy, be good, be good. That's all I ask."

"Competitor?" said the man at the entrance. "Go right in."

In a small ring donkeys were being judged in the showing class. Some of them were no bigger than Tammy; some were chocolate coloured, others grey, a few almost oatmeal. There were crowds of spectators, girls in gay frocks, men in shirt-sleeves, children chattering like monkeys. There were bookies erecting their stalls, and ice-cream vendors in stained white coats, and the smell of hot trampled grass beneath a tireless sun. And through it all he saw the face of Jane, cool and assured and laughing.

"You've got here! Oh, good for you! Why didn't you say you were riding? I've got friends on the way. They could have put you up."

Duggie was overjoyed to find her waiting for them. Together they watered Tammy and tied him beneath a chestnut tree and thought he was shy because he didn't bray to the other donkeys. Duggie wanted to introduce him to a little hinny, but Jane said he mustn't form any attachments till after the race.

In the secretary's tent they collected Duggie's number, which was 27, and had to be tied round the waist.

"That's a lucky one," said the man behind the counter. "What, only in one race?"

"Just the big one," said the boy.

"Why don't you go to the jockey's pool? You'll get another mount. They're short of riders. Are you any good? Done it before?"

"No, but I can gallop all right. I've practised," said Duggie.

"He's jolly good," added Jane.

"Here, Mr. Thomson, weren't you looking for a jockey?" asked the secretary for the day, as a tall farmer came into the tent.

"Yes, why?"

"Here's your boy."

"Can you ride, son?" asked the man.

"He's good," said Jane. "But he's booked for the big race."

"Come out and try my animal, will you?"

It was a chocolate donkey with a white muzzle and pale linings to his ears.

"I paid a fiver for him. He was ill-treated coming over from Ireland on the boat. You should have seen him, all ribs, and his head dragging on the ground. I've got my other one entered for the big race with my daughter riding."

"He's nice," said Duggie, "and bigger than Tammy."

"I'd like you to ride him in the Farmers' Stakes, and I'll give you a pound to do it and two quid if you win. All right?"

"I'll love it," said Duggie.

"Get on and ride him round and let's see how you perform."

Although taller, the chocolate donkey had a shorter stride than Tammy, and his head carriage wasn't as good. Duggie could tell at once that he was less obedient. He walked him for a few minutes and then gave him a brisk canter in a circle and came back to the farmer.

"All right. Fine. He doesn't go any better for my daughter and that's saying something. She's got him in the other races he's entered in. His name's Kitcat, by the way."

"It's an unusual name," laughed Jane.

"Yes, for a donkey," Mr. Thomson replied, looking at the girl with approval.

The first race was about to begin. The bookies were shouting out the odds. People were laying their bets. The commentator was describing the seven entries walking round the paddock.

"You're in the next one, Duggie. Come on, it's time we thought about weighing in."

"I'll look after Kitcat," Jane offered.

He met other jockeys as he weighed in, two small boys like himself, one wearing shorts. "What are you riding?" they asked him. "Brockhampton Wanderer is the one to back to-day. You should have seen him last year. Coo, that donkey can go!"

He wished Old Jock would arrive and was glad of the absence of Mark and Angela. They were not as calm as Jane. They would fuss him. He had never expected the event to be taken so seriously by everyone. He saw people betting in fivers, and the commentator's voice was as professional as anyone reporting a big race over the wireless.

Lots of the donkeys seemed to have lost their humbleness; they were smart and lively and aware of all the eyes resting on them and their importance to-day.

Jane said, "Do you remember that poem, Duggie, 'Fools, for I also had my hour, one fast fierce hour and sweet. There was a shout about my ears and palms before my feet'?"

"Yes, you said it was by the poet, Chesterton. But it doesn't seem to fit some of these. Look at that one." He pointed to a long-legged stallion dragging his

121

owner across the race-ground. "I wonder if he's Brockhampton Wanderer."

The first race had started. They watched the entries bound into a canter on the smooth mown turf of the half-moon course, fenced with white rails. The crowd were cheering as though their lungs would break and stamping their feet or banging their elbows against their sides.

The riders' faces were mostly set and grim. Pounds were in the balance. And only one smiled as she rode. Suddenly a pale-coloured donkey jibbed and a little girl in a brown crash cap and jodhpurs shot over his head and landed hands first in the grass. People began to laugh; some of the tension lessened. The others went on in a bunch, a tall grey leading; then all at once a small donkey at the back began to catch up the other ones, his little legs going like clockwork, his huge ears lying flat on his neck, his rider flapping her legs and arms like a windmill. The crowd began to yell again.

"Come on, Flyaway. Come on, Flyaway!"

"Look out for him in the next race, Duggie. See how he slipped into the inside, next to the rails? That girl's a wizard," said Mr. Thomson.

Flyaway overtook the oatmeal-coloured donkey, a brown stallion and a nondescript grey; another entry suddenly jibbed; the girl's legs flapped harder, the cheering rose to a tumult and she flashed past the winning post, first by two lengths. "Well ridden!" cried Mr. Thomson, and then, lowering his voice, "There's a twenty minute interval between the races. We'll go to the paddock in ten. Here's my daughter. Mary, this is Duggie Brown. He's riding Kitcat in the next race, and he's come all the way from London."

"Goodness," said Mary, and Duggie noticed her

122

sticking-out teeth and her pale skin, and her firm hands on the reins.

Chapter Sixteen

"And what will you be doing on another donkey?" Old Jock was here suddenly, pale and town-like in the country sunlight.

"I've been offered a mount, and it will get me used to the course," said Duggie. Then he saw the woman in front of him open a programme, and the words "Tam o' Shanter," and then "Mark Allington" and "rider, Douglas Brown." And he knew "Jock Mac-Donald" should have been written on that page.

"Come and see Tammy. Duggie's got to go into the paddock now," said Jane. "It will be good for him to have a ride."

"Did you have a good journey over here?" Old Jock asked without moving.

"Fine," said the boy. "I spent last night in a barn just as you said I would."

"We must go to the paddock. Come on," said Mary.

The woman with the programme walked away to lay a bet.

"Kitcat is an outsider. Never raced here before," a man said to a young woman with freckles on her arms.

"Who's Tam o' Shanter? Comes from London," a querulous voice inquired.

"Probably never seen a race-course in his life," someone replied.

The paddock was fenced with white rails, too. Mr. Thomson led Kelpie, his daughter's mount. Flyaway was just in front of Duggie and Kitcat. He was a well-made donkey, compact and strong with plenty of depth; he looked a stayer.

The commentator said Kitcat was a handsome dark-brown donkey in excellent condition, very calm, with an experienced-looking jockey from London. An outsider owned by the well-known farmer, Mr. George Thomson, who had won the stakes last year with Kelpie.

Jane appeared suddenly and said, "Good luck. Old Jock's giving Tammy another grooming."

And then they were going down to the start and people were being cleared out of their way.

"Two to six on Kelpie, three to one on Flyaway, eight to one on Kitcat," called a bookie.

"I like the chocolate one. Mummy, can I put six-pence on Kitcat?" cried a small girl.

"There goes Flyaway. 'E's a good 'un, a real smasher," said a youth in his late teens, casting an empty cigarette packet into the grass with the care-lessness of a Cockney.

"Try to get on the inside,' said Mr. Thomson for the third time. "If he thinks of jibbing, shout at him."

There were eight other entries, and Duggie hardly looked at them; all his attention was on keeping Kit-cat up to his bridle. The line-up was orderly. There was only one false start and then they were off, thirty-two legs going for all they were worth. Duggie held back, waiting for a chance to get on the inside. Kelpie was just ahead, neck-to-neck with Flyaway, and half a length beyond them the favourite, Nankie Pooh, was giving his boy jockey a good ride, and getting tremen-dous encouragement from the crowd. Suddenly Jane's voice rang out, "Go on, Duggie, Kitcat, Kitcat, Kitcat!" and then Mr. Thomson's, "Kelpie, Kelpie. Come on, Mary. Ride him, ride him, ride him!" And at that second Duggie saw his chance; he got on the inside, about thirty yards before the straight run to the winning post. He overtook Kelpie and Flyaway and now there was only Nankie Pooh, a big light-grey donkey with a very white stomach and clipped like a horse. The jockey looked back and saw Duggie's challenge. He edged Nankie Pooh closer to the rails, the crowd cheered and cheered again. Duggie was streamlined with his donkey; he felt his legs were working like mad, his mouth was set. Kitcat's head drew level with Nankie Pooh's pale flank. The winning post was only ten yards away now. Suddenly Duggie heard Mark's voice yell his name—the same voice which had hailed the taxi on that dark night weeks before. The boy turned his head. Had the man met Old Jock yet? For five seconds Duggie's body relaxed, his legs ceased urging, and in those fatal moments Kitcat stopped with a suddenness which sent the boy shooting over the chocolate head on to the resilient turf, hands spread out breaking his fall, saving his face. Kelpie flashed by and then Flyaway, and the crowd yelled and yelled like maniacs in mad glee, and the race was lost. All was over as he vaulted on to his mount again. The cheering died, the crowd hurried from the rails towards the bookies and Duggie knew the first anticlimax of his life.

"Little devil, jibbing at the very last moment. You rode a wonderful race, son. I never knew he had the speed in him," said Mr. Thomson, and the boy realised that only he knew why the donkey had stopped. No one at the rails could have seen those five seconds of inattention.

"Sorry I didn't win, sir," he said.

"Not your fault. The donkey's still green. Here's

the pound and thanks. I'm sorry I haven't entered him in the big race now."

Mark and Angela appeared then. "Jolly bad luck," they said. "You rode a wonderful race. But it wasn't Tam o' Shanter, was it? Where is he? We're dying to see our entry."

"Look, see that man in the herringbone coat? He's Old Jock. I haven't told him about the ten pounds being lost. He doesn't know anything about you, and he hasn't bought the programme or whatever it is yet. Please let Jane explain. He likes her."

He could see distrust crossing Mark's pale, lined face. The man was wondering whether Duggie was a fraud after all, whether he had kept the money for himself.

"All right. But who is Jane?" Angela asked.

"If you lose the old man need never know if he doesn't get hold of a card. Perhaps you mean to lose," said Mark, watching Duggie's face.

"Of course I don't. I want to do my best. I wouldn't have practised so much otherwise. You ask Jane. Here she is."

The librarian came across at that moment in her frock of blue candy stripe, looking gayer and younger than in London, with the seriousness which so often drew her brows together gone from her face.

"Jane, these people have helped me out of a tight spot. I didn't know which way to turn. Please tell them I shall try to win the race. And they've got something to explain too."

He hurried away then leaving them to it, and found Old Jock feeding Tammy with some oats he had brought in an old sack in the train.

"Going to back anything in the next race?" asked the boy, feeling laden anew with guilt.

"No, but I've put five pounds on our friend here. I

126

reckon he could beat any of those which ran in the last race. He's ten to one—the longest odds of all." The man's cheeks were flushed now with excitement. Soon he would see a programme seller and know the truth. Duggie did not want to face him here alone in those circumstances. He prayed that Jane might break the news gently.

"I would not have thought I would live to own a racehorse. Och no, not in my wildest dreams. Ah weel, we never know what is coming to us." A cackle of laughter came from somewhere at the back of his throat. His way of talking always became more Highland when he was excited or distressed. The London English which spattered his conversation would recede into the background. Duggie knew this change as a sign of his mood.

"I've got a pound and I want to put it on Kitcat in the race after the sulky ones, but I don't know whether children can. Will you do it for me, please?"

"Yes," said Old Jock, "I'll be doing that for you. So he gave you a pound did he? If you will be winning the race on my donkey there will be fifty pounds in your pocket I'm thinking."

The boy gave an empty laugh. Why didn't I tell him at the time, he reproached himself. He's got five pounds to bet with and paid his train fare here. He can't be as poor as I thought, though he can't have much. He might have wanted to pay the tenner all over again. Cowardice never pays. Funks are the unhappiest people in the world. They let everyone down. Suddenly Duggie was very ashamed. He fell silent and Old Jock asked if he was nervous.

"Not really. I feel a bit weak. It's watching all those other races which has done it."

"I am thinking we were right to keep Tammy for the one big race. Och, we do not want our donkey to

127

be tired before the hundred guineas." Old Jock straightened his back and looked at the little animal with pride. "He's a fine wee donkey and there's none better here to-day."

The gnarled hands were shaking a little with excitement and the veins stood out hard and blue. Duggie thought he had never seen him so animated and wondered suddenly what he had been like as a boy.

"I will be getting a racecard presently. Now, remember, lad, you must not be mounting all at once. Let me lead the donkey round the paddock a few times first."

"O.K. Will he be all right now? I can't do anything more?"

"No, thank you."

Duggie went back to the rails then to watch the donkeys racing in the light, specially-made sulkies. The drivers looked funny perched up on their tiny seats, crouched forward with earnest faces as though to win was a matter of life and death. Mr. Thomson took a first with Kelpie and Flyaway had a third, and Brockhampton Wanderer, a strongly-built stallion, won the next class with two lengths to spare. Shall have to watch out for that one in the big race, Duggie thought.

The bookies were chalking up the odds for the next and last event before the hundred guineas, as he went back. Kitcat was six to one.

"I laid your bet. Tammy's had forty minutes to digest. You will be better walking him round now. There's not much of a canter up to the start, I'm thinking," said Old Jock, trying to keep the excitement out of his voice.

There was no programme in his hand or pocket as far as the boy could see. The moment had not come yet. It still was up to Jane to break the news which Duggie was afraid to tell.

The race was drawing nearer. He polished the bridle again before he put it on the donkey. No one else rode in blinkers. He would be very noticeable in this brass-laden tack. He felt a sudden deadly calm, an inertia of body, a don't care attitude. The commentator was describing the entries in the next event going up to the start. Kitcat was looking very tired; he said. Duggie kept seeing Mark's face again, the frown of disbelief on the high brow with the widow's peak. It hurt the boy to think he was distrusted; once people suspected you of telling lies there was nothing you could do verbally. Only deeds counted. Only the race in fact.

The commentator told the jockeys for the big race to go to the weighing-in tent. Duggie met the labourer and his family on his way there.

"We've put five bob each way on you. The kids are mad with excitement," the wife said.

"Good luck," said Pauline. "I'm going to go and kiss your donkey."

Duggie saw her when he came back kissing another grey donkey. He vaulted on Tammy and gave him a pipe opener, a quick hand gallop on an empty piece of ground. The commentator announced that Kitcat had won the last race by a neck.

Duggie met Jane and she promised to collect his winnings and put them on Tammy for him. He avoided Angela and Mark which he knew was unfair, because they had come to the rescue and sponsored Tammy without really knowing him at all. But just as he was going into the paddock, Mark called, "We've put a pound each way on you on the strength of that pipe opener," and Duggie knew Jane had done her best with them.

Old Jock led the donkey; his face was grey and his

129

eyes tired, and he looked like something which has crawled out from under a stone on the first day of spring. But Duggie thought only of the race now. His inertia had gone: there was that feeling in the pit of his stomach again and a sort of grim determination which kept him calm. He remounted the donkey. Brockhampton Wanderer was prancing round the paddock. He seemed completely untired by his two races. Kelpie walked with a brisk firm tread, and Flyaway had a wise look about him as though he knew how to win this time. Now Nankie Pooh came in with pride in his bearing and keen eyes which took in the other entries, as though they were nothing to worry about.

"What are you riding now?" his jockey asked.

"Tammy; he's never raced before. He pulls a cart in London."

"I noticed the blinkers. He won't be much good if he's new to the game."

"Don't be so cocky. He's all right," said Old Jock, with an edge to his voice. "Now, lad, get a good start. That's important. You've drawn a good place, second on the inside. You're lucky. You should be winning to-day, I'm thinking."

"It's chance," said Duggie tensely.

"Now you are talking nonsense. It will be your riding which will be winning or losing the race," Old Jock said. "And there's money on you, fifteen pounds of mine. Don't forget it."

This was a new person, speaking with so much irritability in his voice. It wasn't the man to whom he was accustomed.

"I can only do my best," the boy said.

"You can do your utmost."

"Well, my utmost then."

"Don't you be letting people cramp you against the rails again, and I will not be allowing you to fall off this time," said Old Jock, and then mercifully the commentator started his work and their attention turned to his views on the entries for this, the big race of the day.

"The donkeys are in the paddock now. Nankie Pooh, the favourite, looking very sprightly, not tired at all, and his jockey, Andrew Waters, looking very confident. Then Kelpie, a small donkey, well known for his win in the Farmers' stakes last year, in the pink of condition, bright-eyed, hard and fit. Now comes Tam o' Shanter, a little grey animal, very small but with a long stride and good carriage, ridden by Douglas Brown from London who had such bad luck on Kitcat earlier in the day, and then Flyaway. . . ."

"You will be watching the tap dropping carefully, you will not look the other way, will you, lad?" Old Jock asked.

"No, I've practised such a lot," said Duggie with impatience. What was wrong with the old man to-day?

A few minutes later they were going up to the start, eleven of them—the two which had been in every race so far looking very tired.

"Good luck, Duggie," said Mary.

"Good luck, Mary," said Duggie.

"Don't get pushed out at the corner," called Mark.

"Keep him on his toes at the start," advised Jane, leaning over the rails.

The sun was very hot now; it burned through the boy's shirt to his skin, and his London face smarted and he felt sweat trickling down his body. His calmness had gone and he thought Tammy would never leave the start.

131

The words of the boy on Nankie Pooh rang in his ears. "He won't be much good if he's new to the game . . ." Old Jock would never accept that excuse. If I had known the man was going to take it so seriously I would never have entered, Duggie thought.

He knew he would fall off in the first twenty yards now. It was impossible that he would get to the end of that short course without mishap this time. His legs were limp like wet sacking and his brain useless and his arms were like string. They were all there watching. . . . Old Jock, Mark, Angela, Jane, the labourer and his family. They had laid their bets on him. They had come miles to watch him win the race. Surely there was no other jockey to-day with so much responsibility? But it was his own fault. He had wanted to ride in the race, had been certain of Tammy's speed. And how high most of the donkeys seemed now! Brockhampton Wanderer and Nankie Pooh were giants beside Tammy, and Kelpie was nearly a hand taller. His hopes fell lower. But, after all, it was only a race.

Now they were lining up. The moment, of which he had dreamed so often, was here in reality. The limpness left his legs; his arms became stronger and suddenly his brain was calm and clear. He watched the white flag. Flyaway was on his inside: Kelpie was next to him. He heard Jane's urgent voice saying, "Keep him on his toes," and Old Jock's "Good luck." Tammy didn't bray to the other donkeys. He seemed to judge Duggie's mood and to know he was to leap into a gallop at any moment. All the practising had not been in vain.

The white flag was raised. Nankie Pooh made a false start and they had to line up all over again. Duggie heard the commentator's voice, "Coming up again now . . . Brockhampton Wanderer very much on his toes. Tam o' Shanter looking very perky . . ."

Then suddenly, with the suddenness for which they had been waiting, the tape dropped and they were off, and Tammy's plunge forward had put him in second place, behind Flyaway, and his little legs were taking big strides, and his short neck was stretched out as far as it would go. The turf beneath his hoofs was soft. The crowd was cheering and shouting, twelve deep . . . "It's Flyaway and Tam o' Shanter, Flyaway and Tam o' Shanter, then Nankie Pooh, Kelpie and Wanderer, and Beechnut coming up very fast behind. Now they are coming to the bend and it's still Flyaway and Tam o' Shanter, and Tam o' Shanter is gaining, Tam o' Shanter only a neck behind now. Nankie Pooh creeping up. They are all three in a bunch together, Flyaway, Tam o' Shanter and Nankie Pooh . . ." Jane and Old Jock heard the commentator's voice, listened to it, but not Duggie. His ears were oblivious of sound, his eyes conscious only of Flyaway's grey ears and the green course ahead, and the bend which he couldn't take right on the inside. The girl rivalling him was riding with all she had, arms, legs, body. Sweat glistened on the donkeys' coats; their breath shortened; their pace slowed a little on the bend, and then suddenly Flyaway lost ground, Tammy's white muzzle shot ahead. He edged nearer to the rails; he was on the inside, a length in the lead. Flyaway's breath came in a sob.

"Tam o' Shanter in the lead! Tam o' Shanter a length ahead and going strongly, not looking tired. Flyaway dropping back, and now it's Nankie Pooh, Nankie Pooh coming up. Now they're level, Nankie Pooh and Tam o' Shanter, Kelpie just behind, then Beechnut, Flyaway, Wanderer and Whynot, Nankie Pooh and Tam o' Shanter coming into the straight, neck and neck. It's a race . . . Tam o' Shanter gaining. No, Nankie Pooh challenging him again. Nankie Pooh challenging Tam o' Shanter . . ."

The crowd's cheering rose to a frenzy, "Nankie Pooh, Nankie Pooh!" No one knew the donkey from London, the little grey one.

"Come on Tammy!"

The boy on the stallion was using his hands on the animal's pale sides; his voice was threatening him; his face was scarlet, and now Nankie Pooh was overtaking Tammy on the outside and they were tearing down the last straight run before the winning post, and Kelpie was creeping up behind; his muzzle was visible to the boy. I should have kept some energy back, not used it all up at the beginning, Duggie thought, I've been fighting in the lead too long. Nankie Pooh was a length ahead.

"Tam o' Shanter dropping back, looking very tired now. Nankie Pooh in the lead, Nankie Pooh a length ahead from Tam o' Shanter, Kelpie coming up, and Beechnut and now Wanderer, Wanderer coming up very fast, very fast indeed. Wanderer challenging Tam o' Shanter. It's Nankie Pooh, Wanderer and Tam o' Shanter and only forty yards to go. They're all in a bunch now. Nankie Pooh has stopped. Nankie Pooh has dug his toes in, and his jockey is off. Andrew Waters on the ground, unhurt. Now Kelpie, Flyaway, Beechnut and Whynot have overtaken him, and Apple Pie, Jinks and Paddy-Mac way behind them. Brockhampton Wanderer and Tam o' Shanter fighting it out, dead level as two donkeys can be, Kelpie lying third, Wanderer and Tam o' Shanter still level. Wanderer gaining a little. No, now Tam o' Shanter, Tam o' Shanter gaining, the little donkey a neck ahead, his jockey looking very tired. Now it's Wanderer again, and there's only fifteen yards to go . . . Wanderer, Tam o' Shanter."

"Tammy, come on, Tammy," Duggie's voice urged involuntarily. The donkey was slowing down; his breath was coming in gasps. Then a pony's neigh rang out high and clear in the summer air and the little grey legs quickened; the small hocks went farther under the body. They began to gain again. They were level with the rival jockey. Tammy's muzzle crept up to Wanderer's neck. The jockeys were level. They were fighting it out in the last seven yards.

"Brockhampton Wanderer and Tam o' Shanter making a great race of it! Neck and neck again! The little donkey showing amazing stamina! Neck and neck. It's Brockhampton Wanderer and Tam o' Shanter, fighting it out! Now they are there. Going by the winning post. Tam o' Shanter. No, it's Wanderer. They've past. A dead heat. It looked like a dead heat between Brockhampton Wanderer and Tam o' Shanter. And here comes Kelpie, Kelpie third, and then Beechnut and Whynot, Flyaway, Nankie Pooh, Apple Pie, Jinks and Paddy-Mac, Stormy, and a long way behind, led by their jockeys, Mollie and Melanie who jibbed earlier on. Now it's for the judges. The numbers haven't gone up yet. It looked to me from here like a dead heat between Brockhampton Wanderer, well known in this district and a popular runner, and the outsider from London, Tam o' Shanter, with Kelpie third, Beechnut fourth, and then Whynot, Flyaway, and Nankie Pooh remounted by jockey Waters, in that order. A great race and the little Londoner put up a great fight . . ."

Duggie leapt off and covered Tammy with pats. Now Jane and Old Jock were here with beaming excited faces and, in the background, Angela and Mark.

"You may have won sixty pounds, Duggie," said Jane. "I've told Old Jock about the Smithsons. It's all right, so don't worry."

"Get on again. I'm going to lead my winner in," the old man said.

"Congratulations," said Mark.

"You were wonderful, Duggie," added Angela.

"I'm going to give the money to Old Jock," the boy said, under his breath.

"But we've only tied. Will it be half that?"

"The numbers are going up now," the commentator began. "Yes, it's a dead heat, a dead heat between Brockhampton Wanderer, the well-known donkey, owned by Frank Maggs, from Friarfields, Sussex, and Tam o' Shanter, the outsider from London, owned by Mr. Jock MacDonald of Markham Street . . ."

"Mr. Allington asked them to announce Old Jock as the owner," Jane whispered. "You only put the sponsors and yourself on the entry form. There might have been a mistake."

"Come on, lad. It's the only winner I've ever had in my life, and I'm going to lead him in," the old man said.

"I knew 'e was a good 'un, as soon as I saw 'im this morning," the farm labourer's voice came to them, as they started across the green trampled turf, with two thousand pairs of eyes watching them go.

Chapter Seventeen

THERE WAS plenty of room for the four of them in the Ford Consul, driving through the May dusk. Duggie, sitting in the back with Angela, fell asleep and dreamed of haystacks and a weasel leaping through the grass.

They stopped for dinner at a white-washed hotel called the Red Dragon, and Old Jock, over a glass of whisky, refused again to accept a penny from Duggie or Mark.

"I have money from my own bet, and I am an old man. I will not be needing it as you youngsters will. It's enough for me that my donkey won the race and I led the winner in," he said.

Duggie longed to say, "Tied." But the old man wouldn't have it that way. His eyes had seen Tammy pass the post first. It should have been a photo finish, he insisted, then his donkey would have been rightly proclaimed the winner—but there had been no camera there. He wouldn't accept the judges' verdict of a dead heat. Duggie realised for the first time that he was a very obstinate old man.

There was clear soup, and sparkling white table cloths, and large white napkins, and a panelled dining-room. The grown-ups drank wine, and said, "Here's to Tam o' Shanter and his gallant jockey, Douglas Brown."

They raised their glasses and drank to the boy and the donkey.

It's all over and Angela and Mark have won fifty guineas, and Old Jock won't accept a penny from any of us—only this celebration dinner and Tammy's train fare home, thought Duggie watching the grown-ups' happy faces across the table. It's been the best day of my life, he decided, and then he thought of the little grey donkey grazing in the green meadow which a nearby farmer had lent him for the night, with a tall oak in one corner, under which Tammy could stand for shelter.

Mark was talking. "You see, it's my future sister-in-law's car. She's just had a baby and she's not driving again yet, so she lent it to me for the day. It's a pity Jane couldn't come and join in our celebrations too. It's all wrong that the trainer isn't here. Let's see, Mr. MacDonald, you're roast chicken and green peas, aren't you?"

"Your sister-in-law's baby will be about the same age as young Duggie's new sister then," observed Old Jock, leaning towards his plate.

In the car again, the boy thought once more of the Smithsons. He didn't care about the ten pounds now that the race was over. He didn't want revenge; he wanted to be friends with everyone. He was looking forward to seeing Rosemary again. Would she have grown in his four days of absence?

"It's been a fine day this Whitsun," Old Jock said, and Duggie, seeing the man's face by the light of a passing car, thought he looked younger than ever before. There was something almost boyish about the enthusiasm in his expression at that moment, and his laugh had lost its cackle.

"I wish you'd take some of the fifty quid," Mark said for the third time.

"Och, what will I be wanting with that money? Keep it, lad, use it for your honeymoon."

"Tired, Duggie?" asked Angela.

"A little bit."

"I expect Tammy is, too!"

"There's a grand donkey for you."

The suburbs of London were bright with lamplight, and rowdy with revellers, and the roads thick with returning motorists. And now the car crawled and Duggie slept again, until a voice said:

"Wake up! Hi, this is Stroughton Street."

And then he came to with a jerk, not knowing where he was and who spoke. And his father was there opening the car door and saying, "We got Miss Howard's telegram, came just ten minutes ago," and looking awkwardly at Mark and Angela.

"Just made a pot of tea," he added at last. "If you are thirsty, and there's a bottle of beer or two."

They all came in for a few minutes then, and Mark talked to Mr. Brown about the railways and nationalisation, and Angela was invited into the bedroom to see Rosemary, who had just wakened for a feed.

"I didn't know Jane sent a telegram," Duggie said.

"She told me. She's a fine lass," Old Jock remarked, passing a shaky hand across his hot flushed face. "It's been a grand day and it will be doing the donkey good to be resting in the country till Wednesday. Mr. Allington is a fine gentleman, I'm thinking."

"Here's my address, Duggie, in case you ever need anything. I want you to come to tea one Saturday

139

with my mother and Mark," said Angela, writing on the back of a crumpled post-card.

"Now it's all over, son. You've got to work for that there examination," said Mr. Brown. "Here, take that cup of tea to Jennifer, she's woke up."

Angela and Mark took Old Jock away with them at eleven.

As Duggie climbed the cream staircase he knew the day was really over, the dream ended with greater happiness all round than he had dared to hope. In bed, with the glow from the street lamp familiar across the bare boards, he slept the dreamless sleep of true content.

In the morning he wakened late, and his mother scolded him for the way he had kept the race a dark secret. Pete and Dick came to congratulate him, and Mrs. Towers called her best wishes to him from her open window.

He told his mother of the money he had won and offered to buy clothes for his brother and sister and to help furnish the new flat when they got it. But she said his winnings must go into the post office, to be used when he was older. Duggie remembered Jane saying, "It will come in useful if you do get to an agricultural college. You'll need every penny you've got then," and he was grateful to his mother for not accepting the money for the others, although he was going to buy them each a present with five pounds of it. No one would persuade him out of that.

He thought again of Old Jock's sudden generosity and his kindness when Jane had told him the fate of his ten pounds. The man seemed no longer to care for money, to have become, suddenly, a nobler person.

It was evening when the boy made his way at last to the basement room, climbed down the damp chipped steps and smelt the dustbins in the shed

140

nearby. It was very quiet and still. Not even a car passed by. He opened the door slowly and carefully, frightened suddenly by the silence.

The old man was lying in bed and his face was ashen.

"Here you are. I've been waiting a long time for you to come. Will you be doing one more thing for

"Will you be doing one more thing for me, Douglas Brown?"

me, Douglas Brown?" His voice was no more than a croak.

The boy crossed the room with faltering footsteps. "What's that?" he asked with greater brusqueness than he meant, shocked by the voice and the man, remembering the glowing cheeks of only twenty-two hours ago, the firm hand on the whisky glass, the smile of triumph on the old wrinkled face.

"Can you see the hole by the seam of my under

mattress? Will you be taking this knife and opening it wider? That's right, lad, cut where it's tacked."

The boy's hands were quick and the knife sharp. The red and white tacking came apart, showing the coarse stuffing beyond.

"Put your fingers inside, lad, and feel until you come against something flat and hard. That's the way. Now pull, gently, gently, just a wee while harder. Here she comes."

Duggie brought out a square flat box about two feet by two. He felt in a dream, far from reality.

"It's still safe then. It was a good secret and the bed was mine and only my sister Alison knew. It's a fine strong box to be sure, and I forgetting it was brown."

"What's in it?" Duggie asked, growing impatient with the man's wandering mind.

"You will be seeing in a wee while. Now fetch the coat from the door for me," croaked the tired, unfamiliar voice.

The room was musty and the window dark with grime, and the view of the dustbins was a drear scene for the eyes. Duggie felt a wave of depression as he crossed the room again. He wished the old man had accepted the money he had offered him; it would have paid for the window to be cleaned and for new curtains and brighter furniture.

He brought back the familiar overcoat and the old man took a small key from an inside pocket and held it between finger and thumb.

"You rode a fine race yesterday. He's a grand donkey and I'm awful glad I was there to see it. Mr. Allington is a fine shentleman and the lassie a fine lady, and I'm right glad they had the money, so you will never need to be worrying about the ten pounds the boys took from you." As he spoke he looked at

142

the box as though he could hardly bear to open it. He wore a worn nightshirt, pale as his skin, and his eyes tried to smile with his mouth, and his voice was like a frog's croak, so that Duggie only wanted to burst into tears and dash from the room into the street.

"I wish, I wish you could have known my wee wife, Douglas Brown. You would have loved her, I'm thinking. She was a grand lassie. If the good Lord had not taken her, we would have retired to the country. But I could not retire without her, you will understand, I could not, and seventy-seven I am this year."

His hand reached out with the key. "Undo the lock in the box, and count the money and you will have my gratitude," he said, leaning forward with sudden urgency.

The key made a little grinding sound in the lock, and then the flat lid came up and there below were scores of one pound notes, some old and dirty, some crisp and clean. Duggie stared.

"Pound notes. Have you not seen the like of them before? Count them and I will be grateful to you for the service."

He had not been poor then, not poor at all. The boy put them in piles of ten with shaking hands, and, as he worked, the old man lay back and closed his eyes and for a moment there was only the rustle of the thin paper and the breathing of the two humans to break the silence in the room. It seemed like a nightmare.

Then a car went by and there was the sound of children shuffling their feet in the road, and the shrill bark of a dog and, farther away, the whistle of a train near Paddington Station.

"Put them in piles of twenty and it will be saving you time." Old Jock stirred as he spoke and pulled himself up on to one elbow. "How many are there, lad, how many?"

The piles were stretching all across the brown linoleum floor and on the rag mat by the oak table—little ineffectual heaps of crisp white paper. "I'm counting," the boy answered, crawling on his hands and knees, putting the heaps in line.

"One hundred piles," he said at last. "It's an awful lot."

"And how much would that be? Two thousand pounds would you be thinking?"

"Yes, that's the amount, Mr. MacDonald," said Duggie a moment later, afraid to use the famliar "Old Jock" to one so rich.

"Thank you. Now would you be so kind as to put the money back in the box, lock it up and give the key to me."

It seemed a waste to pick up his neat rows, but he did as he was told, his brain in a maze of unbelief.

"Did you make it all from rags and bones?" he asked at last.

"Yes, but it's not a lot of money, I'm thinking. There's many make more, but I was always fond of the whisky on a cold night."

When the box was once again full and locked, the old man asked that it should be put beneath his pillow.

"Now, there's one more wee thing I'm wanting to tell you. The donkey's yours. I'm giving him to you and I know that you will be looking after him well, and caring for him as he deserves."

"But, but . . ." began Duggie.

"Och, no buts and no questions. The donkey's yours. Can you understand that?"

"Thank you," said Duggie, lost for further words.

"Now get me that old pen and the piece of paper from the drawer in the table. That's right. Put the old cushion behind my back. Are you frightened? Would you be afraid?"

"No," said Duggie not understanding. "Can I go and get a doctor, or the people from above?"

"And that's just what I was wanting you to do. Will you go now, Douglas Brown, to Higher Hornton Street, number 23, and be kind enough to tell Dr. Cameron to come here and to see Old Jock Mac-Donald, who came from his own land in the Western Highlands where he grew up as a boy."

"Supposing he's out?"

"Well then, his wife or the housekeeper will be getting in touch with Dr. Macpherson, I'm thinking." He paused. "Now, go, and good-bye, and look after the donkey for me," he croaked, and Duggie looked back and saw the white face and the dull blue eyes for the last time. And the knot tightened in his aching throat, and tears came.

Outside the sun turned the clouds to gold, and the birds sang joyfully in the plane trees. Duggie started to run with all the speed that was in him.

Chapter Eighteen

OLD JOCK died in the early hours of the next morning. Dr. Cameron was with him and a Scottish minister.

"Don't cry, Duggie," said Mrs. Towers, meeting the boy in the street after the news had come. "He's happy now with his wife in heaven. He hadn't anything left to live for. You gave him a proud moment, love. He even told the doctor about the race, how you

145

rode and all. He couldn't have gone round the streets again with the donkey, and what could 'e have done all day alone in that room? It's a 'appy release, love. I bet he's 'appy up there with 'is wife at last. 'E loved 'er they say, and was never the same again after she died." She smiled at Duggie and he tried to smile, too, because he knew that what she had said was true. What could the old man have done with himself all day now that he was too old to go on the rounds?

The boy wanted to tell Mrs. Towers about the box of notes, how he had always imagined Old Jock to be so poor and all the time there had been two thousand pounds in his mattress. But he thought the old man might have wanted it kept a secret, so he remained silent. Then he remembered he was to meet Tammy's train at the station at half-past eleven.

He hurried away to get the stall ready, and met Mrs. Tinsel, Old Jock's sister.

"So he's left you the donkey and not the money," she said without any preamble. "The Minister and the doctor witnessed the will he wrote last night. The dog and cat are to be put in the care of Miss Howard. I'm right glad about that—dirty creatures they were, to be sure."

Duggie wondered whether she had opened the flat box yet. Old Jock must have mentioned it in the will; otherwise he would never have wanted the money checked.

"I was with him last night. I counted the notes," he said, after a pause.

"Och, so you know and all. Well, I would be grateful if you would keep your mouth shut on that score, Douglas, or it will be all over the district. These things should be private."

"That's all right, I won't tell anyone," said Duggie,

146

knowing he would never forget those moments in the basement room.

"It's a happy release. He was old and sick. He knew he wouldn't last long when he came out of the hospital. He had had his life," said Mrs. Tinsel.

"I must be going. I have to meet the donkey, if you don't mind, and there's the stall to get ready," the boy said, thinking suddenly of the dog and cat waiting alone. "I'm sorry about it all, Mrs. Tinsel."

Later, at the station, Tammy gave him a bray of welcome, and he looked at the little donkey and thought, he's mine; he belongs to me—my donkey. There was mud on the grey coat, a patch above the left eye which gave the animal a rakish look, and a great blob on the rump which proved he had rolled over and over in the May grass.

Duggie signed a form in the Parcel Office, saying he had received the donkey in good condition, and then he jumped on to Tammy's back and set off for home.

"No more rag and boning for you, no more cold days going from door to door in the rain," he said, and one long ear came back to listen to his words.

Just outside the mews he met Pete and Dick.

"We've heard the news. The donkey's yours," they said. "What are you going to do with 'im?"

"I don't know. I haven't thought. I can't seem to concentrate this morning."

It was true: he couldn't think straight. His mind went round in circles, repeating the same things. . . . Two thousand pounds would you be thinking. . . . The donkey's yours. . . . A happy release. . . . I hear you have a baby sister. . . . I'm going to get you a Council flat. . . . You see, you could go to an Agricultural College if you passed the Eleven plus. . . . Two thousand pounds would you be thinking?

Too much had happened too quickly, but Mrs. Towers had said life was like that, "Never rains, but it pours. You go months, love, without anything 'appening at all and then suddenly it's one thing after another, coming on so fast you don't know what you are doing."

"Seen the Smithsons lately?" asked Pete.

"No, but I've hardly been here the last few days."

"Will you keep the donkey in the mews and ride him before school every morning?"

"I don't think so, Pete. You see, I reckon he loves the country."

He was hearing the birds singing in Peterson's elms again and watching the donkey walk away across the sunlit grass.

"I think he likes the country best. This mews is a dark place for an animal, and it's not right he should be tied up so long."

He thought of the barn and the moonlight, lying silver on the little grey figure in the corner.

"I want him to be happy. He deserves it, and I want him to roll in the grass till he's tired of rolling and to eat as much as he likes and to feel free. He can't do any of that here, Pete."

"And that's a fact," his friend agreed.

Duggie fed and watered the donkey, and the others watched him and then the three of them walked out into the sunlight together.

"I'm glad we get this week's holiday at Whitsun. It breaks the term up. You *are* sitting for the Eleven plus then, Duggie," Dick said.

"That's right." The race seemed years ago now, and Angela and Mark like figures in a dream. He tried to relive it, but instead his mind switched to Rosemary. The wrinkles had left her face now and her eyes would soon be in focus, and he wished he could take her for a ride on the donkey one day. And he thought, one death and one birth all in a few weeks, and tried to imagine Old Jock's brown-eyed wife sitting with a halo round her head somewhere above the cloudless sky.

Now the boys were coming to the corner where the little bay pony stood all day, and suddenly Pete said, "Look." And Duggie raised his eyes from the road, and saw two others boys by the cart and realised with a shock that these were Jim and Frankie.

"Do you want your revenge?" Pete asked. "If they start any funny stuff, we've got David to support us."

The road was empty of pedestrians. It was lunch time. The boys were pretending to admire the pony and cart, but surreptitiously they were filling their pockets with apples and bananas. He saw their hands working with skill, and supposed the costermonger was having a glass of beer in the pub.

"They're stealing," he whispered.

"I can see. Let's stop them. It's wrong," said Dick.

"Look out for drawing-pins. Wonder if they spent that ten pounds? If we get it back will you give me half?" Pete asked.

"You can have it all," said Duggie. He remembered the bump on the head he had suffered, the dizziness he had felt in the evening. "O.K., we'll challenge them," he agreed.

The three boys hurried forward.

"Now, what are you up to? First you steal ten pounds, and then an old man's fruit," said Pete.

The Smithsons started when they heard his voice. Then, when recognition showed on their faces, Jim said, "Oh, so it's you again. I thought we'd taught yer a lesson. Shut yer mouf and stop interfering, can yer 'ear me?"

"I'll fetch a policeman," said Dick, who had none of Duggie's scruples on that score.

"Sssh. Don't do that," said Pete.

"So you'd nark, too, would yer?"

"I never told on you," Duggie said.

"Yer narked about yer ruddy donkey, and poor old George got it. If it hadn't been for that 'e might not have got taken away, see. It was the last thing in the balance, wot turned them finally aginst 'im.'"

"It must have been the woman with the umbrella. It wasn't me. And you had better be careful because there's a woman watching you from the other side of the road," Duggie said.

"Where did he get taken, prison?" asked Pete.

"Mind yer own business," Frankie said.

"You are juvenile delinquents and you ought to be in an approved home," said Dick, looking prim.

"'Ark at 'im. Wot does 'e think 'e is, a school teacher or somefink," jeered Frankie.

Duggie felt outside what was happening. He supposed half of him was still attached to the last week. Nothing the other four boys said seemed of the slightest importance. He didn't really mind if the Smithsons thought he had informed against them, and the stealing of fruit seemed a minor affair measured against his journey to the races, the arrival of Rosemary and the end of Old Jock.

"I'll fetch the police," Dick said again, and to Duggie his voice was like a voice in a cloud.

"I'll clout yer on the lug-'ole first," threatened Frankie.

"You try," said Dick, coming back to life.

Duggie looked at the three scars running down Pete's cheek again. Now he wanted to get his own back for all the Smithson's had done to them, not for the ten pounds in particular—that didn't seem to matter any more.

"Put back that fruit," he said.

At that moment they saw the costermonger behind them.

"So it's you who've been 'elping yourselves, is it?" he shouted and seized Jim by the collar of his coat. "I'll teach you to come pinching my fruit." He put his hands in the boy's pockets and started to pull out the apples and bananas. "You ought to be in a home, that's where you should be."

At that word, Frankie seemed to lose his self control.

"Let 'im go. Let go of Jim, do yer 'ear?" He leapt as he spoke at the old man and punched his face, but the costermonger still held Jim. "Fetch a constable," he said.

Duggie didn't move, nor Pete, but Dick said "O.K." and was running down the street in a moment, and then the Smithsons suddenly started to fight in earnest, fear spurring them on and making them reckless. A knife flashed suddenly in the sunlight; it glanced across the man's cheek and then was raised again to make a deadlier blow. Duggie dashed into the fray.

He got hold of Frankie's arm and tried to force it behind his back, but there didn't seem room. Somehow he was muddled up with the costermonger and Jim. He saw apples rolling into the gutter, and heard Frankie saying, "Run for it, run," under his breath, but neither of the Smithsons could break free now.

Passers-by stopped and stared; the pony whinnied, and the knife came up again as though to slash the costermonger's cheek. And then suddenly a car braked; blue-coated men appeared, policemen, and, somewhere in the background, Dick.

151

They seized Duggie and Frankie by their shirt collars and pulled them roughly from the fray.

"What's going on 'ere?"

"The little one's all right. 'E's wif me. 'E 'elped," said the costermonger. "It's 'im wif the knife. See the blood on me cheek? And the other one." He had Jim in his power now.

"I'm going," said Duggie, as the policeman let him go.

"Been tiking my fruit," the costermonger began.

"Let's get their names first, so we can contact their mothers," a policeman said, bringing out a notebook. "We'll have to take them to the station."

"The little fair 'un's all right. He helped," said a wizened old man who had been watching from the other side of the road.

"See the fruit in their pockets?" asked the costermonger pulling out bananas and apples with which to demonstrate their theft. "And look at this 'ere knife."

Duggie slipped away at that moment, and Pete with him. Dick stayed because he wanted to see what happened. He thought of policemen as friends and didn't mind giving evidence against the Smithsons.

"It wouldn't have been so bad if they hadn't had a knife," Duggie said. "They'll probably go before a court for that. They actually cut the man."

"They've been asking for it for a long time."

"Come home and see how Rosemary's grown," Duggie suggested. "I can't bear to think of Tammy indoors with sun like this. After lunch I shall take him to Charles Crescent and graze him under that tree."

Suddenly he wanted to think only of the nice things in life, his baby sister, the grass and the leafy boughs of May and the donkey which was his, and to forget the Smithsons with their warped minds, and approved schools and criminals. He had had as much as he could take. He felt tears at the back of his eyes.

Chapter Nineteen

"YOU'LL BE able to come and stay here in the summer holidays," said Angela's sister for the third time. "And at Easter, too. And you can help Sandra with her riding, and the farmer next door with his harvest."

They watched the little donkey roll beneath the trees and get to his feet stained with the yellow of the buttercups, with pink blossom on his coat and a blade of grass still between his lips, hanging like a damp cigarette from the mouth of a vague-minded smoker. They saw him wander round the orchard, sniffing the ground and stopping here and there to gaze over the thick hedges, his long ears pricked and his small eyes feasting on the fields basking in May's sunshine.

Duggie was seeing the golden wheatfields, the tall corn falling before the reaper, the combine separating the grain from the straw, the hot sunburnt men with the calm of the country in their eyes. And he heard, in the blueness of night, the footsteps on the road, the labourers going to an old pub to drink the dark beer at the end of their long day, and over the dew-wet meadows the church clock telling the hours and in the dark woods a nightingale.

"It's only fair that you should come and stay in exchange for the loan of the donkey. Sandra is thrilled. There will be a pony in that orchard next week so he won't be lonely," said Angela's sister, her gay educated voice breaking the boy's day-dream.

"That will be lovely, Duggie, won't it?" said Jane, her tone crisp and cool as the grass beneath the apple trees.

Somewhere a jay scolded and a hen clucked to her chicks, and ducks quacked. He collected his thoughts with a jolt.

"Yes. I would like to, thanks. Do you think Jock would be pleased to see Tammy here, wandering in the long grass and with a pony friend next week?" he asked, seeing the dark stall again, the garages in the mews, the long grey street.

"He probably *can* see, and no one could be anything but pleased to watch a donkey in these surroundings. It's the perfect place for semi-retirement, especially after seven years in London," Jane said encouragingly.

"You could take him to the Donkey Derby next year if you wanted to. I could lug him for long walks with Sandra to get him fit," said Angela's sister.

"I believe there's a Donkey Grand National in August. If he jumps he could enter for that," said Jane.

Tammy was rolling again now, his white tummy turned to the clear blue of the skies, his legs kicking the air, his short straight back deep in the grass.

"Mr. Allington was good to put ten pounds on a donkey without seeing him," Duggie said, wondering again at Mark's impulsive generosity.

"He always does mad things like that. He gave a beggar a fiver in Naples once when he had a whacking great overdraft at the bank," said Angela's sister.

"They did go and see Tammy, but no one was there. The man at the garage told them you were all right, and exercising the donkey very carefully. They actu-

154

ally took Tammy out in the mews and had a look at him," said Jane, "Angela told me; it was four days before the race and Mark suddenly wondered whether you were a fraud and there was no donkey at all. He thought there might be still time to stop his cheque—which there wasn't of course."

"Just like Mark. He's so irresponsible," said Angela's sister with a laugh.

Duggie remembering his panic in the wet road and Mark's quick dash into the pub to phone for a taxi, said, "I don't know about that."

As they wandered indoors to eat egg sandwiches and home-made cakes, the boy thought of Jane, too. It had been her idea to ask Angela and Mark whether they knew of anyone who would like the use of a donkey and she had given up her Saturday afternoon to travel down here in the horsebox with Tammy and himself.

He ate in silence, thinking over the events of the last eleven days, and the fate of the Smithsons, who were to come before a juvenile court, and, because their parents were said to be unkind and irresponsible, would almost certainly go to an approved home. There, Jane said, they would learn to be honest and happy. He thought of the elderly woman in the Crescent who allowed Tammy to graze beneath her trees, while Duggie was at school, and saw that he did not go thirsty; and the tall thin master with the rimless spectacles saying, "You'll get through the Eleven plus, Douglas, as long as you keep your head. You've got the brains." And, last of all, he thought of the new Council flat, the four rooms, the bright kitchen and the brand new bathroom, and that wonderful, un-believable view across the rooftops of London, look-ing down on myriad lights and up to the bright stars of heaven.

Except for Jock's death everything has come right, he thought, munching an egg sandwich. Jane said the old man knew he was going to die—he only lived for the race those last days—and he wanted to be with his wife again:

> 'One crowded hour of glorious life
> Is worth an age without a name,'

Jane had quoted, and he remembered Old Jock drinking the red wine and cutting the spring chicken, and saw him again, flushed with triumph as he led his donkey in.

And then Duggie thought of Rosemary, of Jennifer and Fred and the big flat, and he looked out of the window and saw the mauve lilac drooping in the sun, and he heard the low moo of the cows at the farm coming into be milked, and a bee in the herbaceous border. He thought, in August I shall be here; in harvest time, all this will be mine; and now there seemed no limit to his happiness.

OTHER PONY TITLES AVAILABLE IN ARMADA INCLUDE—

ARMADA BOOKS

They are wonderful, with their gay spines adding colour to your bookshelf. Are you collecting your own library of Armada Books? A book a week . . . or a month . . . and in no time you would have a marvellous collection! *Start today!* Always ask your bookseller or newsagent for Armada Books, but if you have difficulty in obtaining the titles you want write to Armada Books, 14 St. James's Place, London, S.W.1, enclosing a postal order to cover the cost of the book(s) and postage (postage to addresses in the U.K. and Ireland—6d. for one book). Overseas readers should write to the same address for information about their nearest stockists, etc.

BOOKS AVAILABLE INCLUDE:

School stories by—

Angela Brazil
Elinor M. Brent-Dyer
Anthony Buckeridge
Frank Richards
Noel Streatfeild
Geoffrey Willans and Ronald Searle
P. G. Wodehouse

Mystery and Adventure stories by—

Christine Bernard
Enid Blyton
John Gunn
Captain W. E. Johns
Ralph Hammond
Alfred Hitchcock
Malcolm Saville

Animal stories by—

Walt Morey
Martha Robinson

AND MANY OTHERS, including some Classics.

For current stock list please send a stamped self-addressed envelope to Armada Books, 14 St. James's Place, London, S.W.1.